# RING OF FIRE

Wellington swung a roundhouse kick into Tom's side with such force that it rolled Tom completely over. Dropping to one knee, the Duke jabbed down with a fierce punch aimed straight between Tom's eyes.

Tom rolled just before the blow connected and countered with a backhand punch that caught Wellington square in the nose. Wellington stood up, dazed, and teetered back. Then he toppled forward on his face and lay still.

A hush fell over the audience. Johnny Weisel, the champ's manager, scurried into the ring and got to Wellington's side.

"Duke!" he shouted, but Wellington didn't respond. He patted his face. Nothing. When Weisel raised his head again, his face was white with horror. He shoved an accusing finger at Tom.

"He's dead!" Weisel screamed. "You killed him!"

# TOM SWIFT

3

## CYBORG KICKBOXER

**VICTOR APPLETON**

**AN ARCHWAY PAPERBACK**
Published by POCKET BOOKS

New York  London  Toronto  Sydney  Tokyo  Singapore

AN ARCHWAY PAPERBACK *Original*

An Archway Paperback published by
POCKET BOOKS, a division of Simon & Schuster Inc.
1230 Avenue of the Americas, New York, NY 10020

Copyright © 1991 by Simon & Schuster Inc.

Produced by Byron Preiss Visual Publications, Inc.
Special thanks to Steven Grant

ISBN: 0-671-67825-6

First Archway Paperback printing June 1991

10  9  8  7  6  5  4  3  2  1

TOM SWIFT, AN ARCHWAY PAPERBACK and colophon
are registered trademarks of Simon & Schuster Inc.

Cover art by Carla Sormanti

Printed in the U.S.A.

IL 6+

# CYBORG KICKBOXER

**A** GLOVED FIST SMASHED INTO TOM SWIFT'S stomach, knocking the wind out of him. The heel of a hand glanced off his temple, detonating a wave of pain that momentarily clouded his vision. Desperately he jabbed out with his fist but struck only air. His opponent was out of his reach, and Tom had the sinking feeling he was easy prey.

His vision began to clear, and he saw a blurry figure hunching in front of him. Tom feinted with a high kick and swiveled quickly on his other foot, out of the way of an onrushing blow. The sleeve of his loose white canvas jacket whipped through the air. The speed and energy of his movement gave him a thrill of power, a promise of invincibility. His punch was dead on, smacking straight into his opponent's jaw.

A split second before impact, Tom saw himself in one of the many mirrors that covered the walls of the room. His opponent had rolled out of the way, and he was about to strike his own reflection. He tried to pull his punch, but his gloved fist smacked against the mirror, sending a jolt up his arm.

In the mirror he saw the enemy behind him. A leg swept around and clipped the backs of Tom's knees, and his legs buckled under him.

He crashed to the thick mat, the thrill of combat crashing with him, and lay there, dazed.

"Had enough?" Rick Cantwell asked, standing over him in a fighting pose. He was dressed in a karate uniform identical to Tom's. Relaxing, Rick swept his sandy brown hair from his eyes and reached out a hand to help Tom up. "I can think of better things to do than beat up on my best friend."

Tom refused the hand. The blow had stung him more than he wanted to let on. He knelt on the mat, tore off his head guard, and took a deep breath. "No, don't stop. Just let me catch my breath."

Rick squatted in front of him, studying Tom's face. Tom wondered what Rick saw there. In the time since Tom's father had moved Swift Enterprises to the quiet California town of Central Hills, Tom Swift and Rick Cantwell had cemented a firm friendship. But while Rick's broad, good-natured face always revealed everything that was on his mind, Tom was much harder to read.

"What's this all about, Tom?"

"I'll tell you soon." Tom flashed a smile and stood, leaning slightly forward with his hands up and ready. "Let's do it."

Rick squared off against Tom, and for a long moment they circled each other. "On," Tom said softly.

"What?" Rick thought he heard a soft electronic hum, but in a massive complex like Swift Enterprises, which covered four square miles, you got used to such sounds. Here were labs and testing grounds that housed gadgets and equipment of great number and variety. The dim noise from them was a constant factor in the complex, even here in the gymnasium.

"Let's go," Tom challenged, and Rick put all other thoughts aside.

He half-jabbed, and Tom caught the blow with his forearm and easily turned it aside.

Rick jabbed again, a little harder. Tom backed out of range. Rick punched with his left, a little wide, and as Tom dodged it, Rick sprang high in the air and whipped his leg around. The high roundhouse kick shot at Tom's head.

Tom ducked and spun, driving his elbow into Rick's back as he landed. Rick staggered and caught his balance, wincing as he straightened up, not from pain but from the suddenness of it all. He stared hard at Tom, trying to get angry.

But Tom's grin spread into laughter at the look on Rick's face, and then they were both laughing.

"You tricked me," Rick said. "You said you'd never done this before, but I can tell someone's been teaching you. Have you been sneaking off to Master Choso's behind my back?"

Tom had been waiting for Rick to bring up Master Choso. It had only been six months since the former world kickboxing champion had retired to Central Hills to teach karate and other martial arts. Rick, always looking to improve his skills as quarterback for the football team at Jefferson High, had been one of Master Choso's first students and had progressed rapidly in the art and sport of kickboxing. Indeed, Master Choso had often spoken of Rick as future championship material.

Now many of the teenagers who attended Jefferson were taking lessons from Master Choso, but Tom's encounters with the martial arts master had been strained. Eager to explore the knowledge, skill, and sheer science involved in kickboxing, Tom soon joined Rick on his visits to Master Choso's dojo, or school. Tom's visits soon stopped. While not at all conceited, Tom was used to respect for his accomplishments. Master Choso, though polite, demonstrated by his curt and routine manner that he had no patience for Tom. Tom soon learned it was a difference of opinion. Master Choso held in cool disdain the advancement-through-technology attitude that Tom's life exemplified, viewing it as a poor substitute for the development of one's natural powers through meditation and discipline. Tom had decided to let things be. Still, the rejection hurt, and Tom was determined to let Master Choso see the virtues of high technology.

"No, I haven't been back to see the master," Tom said. "Off."

At Tom's command the humming stopped. Rick's jaw dropped.

"You invented something!" Rick exclaimed. "I should have guessed. But what could you possibly invent for kickboxing—and why didn't you ask *me* to test it? I thought we were friends!"

"As a matter of fact ..." Tom began. He laughed and then began to peel off his jacket.

On Tom's triceps, shouldercaps, and lower stomach were strings of black disks only an inch in diameter. Wafer thin so they fit flush with his skin, they were held together by a fibrous white mesh that curved snugly against Tom's torso and was as flexible and formfitting as a tight T-shirt. "Beautiful, isn't it?" Tom asked.

"I'll tell you when I know what it is," Rick shot back.

"Okay, okay," said Tom. He peeled a disk from the mesh across his stomach and held it up for Rick to see. "This little baby will revolutionize sports."

"It looks like those things they stick to you in the hospital when they want to keep track of your vital signs."

Tom nodded. "That's the general idea, but it's a lot more complicated than that. There's a microchip in each disk, along with a tiny receiver and electrostatic generator, all mounted on a miniature solenoid."

"Clue me in," Rick said. "How is this supposed to change the face of sports?"

"You apply these to certain muscle groups." Tom carefully pressed the disk back into the mesh covering his abdomen, and it stuck there. "They work like this. See the mirrors on the walls? I created them myself. They're not really mirrors; they're more like huge camera lenses. Any images that hit them immediately get sent to a computer for analysis and storage."

"So you took pictures of us fighting," Rick summarized. "How does that make you a better fighter?"

"Let me explain the entire system. When we started sparring the last time, I switched the system on."

"That was the hum I heard?"

"Right. Then, when you started moving, the computer analyzed your movements. When it calculated the precise move you were making, it scanned its data banks for the countermove. Then it sent a series of signals to the disks I'm wearing, and the disks transmitted the signals through this exoskeleton." Tom rapped his knuckles against the fibrous vest. "It's completely composed of optical fibers. The disks and fiber optics combined to send little shocks into my muscles that caused them to respond with the correct counter-move. Just as your brain shoots signals down your nervous system to tell your muscles what to do."

"Let me see if I've got this straight," Rick said. "You beat me by giving yourself electric shocks?"

"Don't sound so skeptical," answered Tom. "There are belts that work stomach muscles using the same principles, duplicating thousands of sit-ups with controlled electrical charges. I just took it a little further."

"I'll say. Doesn't it hurt, getting little shocks like that?"

"No," Tom said. "It's really pretty invigorating. Want to try it?"

"So that's why you asked me over here," Rick said. He plucked a disk from Tom's shoulder and studied it. "You could wear a shirt over the system, and no one would even know it was there."

"Right. The signal system is completely wireless. The disks store body heat and solar energy, so they generate their own power."

"And if I wore these, I could beat a champion?" Rick asked.

Tom shrugged. "The point isn't to beat people, it's to learn faster. It's one thing to know the right moves, it's another to use them properly at the right time by reflex. Your body has to know, not just your brain. That's what this does: It directly teaches your body what it has to know. And it does it in record time."

Rick could barely contain his excitement. "So it could make me a better football player, too."

"In theory. Any actions that can be videotaped and translated into computer memory can be taught to you as you need them." Tom thought for a moment. "Isolating actions on a busy football field is something I'll have to work on. For now I think I'll have a lot more luck with individual competition sports, like tennis—"

"—or kickboxing," Rick interjected.

Tom nodded. "Which is really pretty complex. It's more complicated than boxing because you fight with your legs, feet, and arms as well as your fists, but it's different from karate because you have gloved hands, so you can't grab and throw anyone, and you can't use chops. It takes a lot of speed, power, and endurance."

"I know all that," said Rick. "So what do you want me to do?"

"I still have a few bugs to work out," Tom said. "I can always use the system on myself, but it would go a lot faster if I could, say, test it out on you."

"I always wanted to be a cyborg!" shouted Rick. "That's what it's like, right? Man and computer, joined as the perfect fighting machine." He looked at the black disk he still held and slapped it onto his forehead with a laugh. Tom laughed, too.

"I don't know if I'd put it quite like that," Tom said, "but, yeah, cyborg is as good a way as any to describe it."

Moving stiffly, as if he were a robot, Rick shadow-kickboxed. "Well, I'm ready. What do we do first?"

"First," Tom said, "we go see Master Choso."

Tom and Rick sat cross-legged on the polished wooden floor of the dojo. Across from them, on a small, plain cotton mat, sat Master Choso, deep in thought. Now in his mid-forties, his hairline receding, his brow etched with deep furrows, he still radiated a sense of calm power.

Abruptly Master Choso stood. Wiry and just under six feet, he seemed muscular, but with clothes on he appeared slight. It was hard to believe he had been a champion fighter. Master Choso signaled Tom and Rick to their feet and opened his shirt, exposing his stomach.

"Hit me," he told Tom, pointing at his waist. Tom glanced uncertainly at Rick.

"Go ahead," said Rick. "He knows what he's doing."

With a deep sigh Tom drove his fist at Master Choso. Something blurred in front of him. Then he was on the floor, his wrist gripped between Master Choso's steely fingers, the man's heel gently placed on his throat. Master Choso helped Tom back to his feet.

"This machine of yours," Master Choso asked, "can it do that? With speed, grace, and accuracy?"

"No," Tom admitted. "But I think it can teach someone to do it."

Again Master Choso lapsed into deep thought. "Yes," he said after a few moments of consideration. "I will help you."

Rick's jaw dropped. "You're serious? But you always said—"

Master Choso waved him silent. "I have always thought the old ways best. But now that I am in America, I must consider new ways." He turned to Tom. "This may turn out to be something of value."

"I hope so," Tom said nervously. There was

something in the man's sly smile that worried him. What did Master Choso really have in mind?

Suddenly the master clapped his hands. A door leading to the next room opened, and through it appeared the biggest man Tom had ever seen.

He was six feet eight and solid muscle, with curly blond hair, which somehow only added to the air of menace about him. His lips curled back into a frightening snarl. He looked as if he could take on an army bare-handed, and his pinched stare fixed on Tom and Rick.

"Do you know who that is?" Rick whispered breathlessly. "Duke Wellington! He's the heavyweight kickboxing champion of the world!"

"I cannot personally take part in your experiments," Master Choso explained calmly. "I hope Mr. Wellington will be a suitable substitute."

As the master spoke, Wellington's face seemed to twist into a barely contained mask of rage. Rick went white as a sheet.

"What's the matter?" Tom whispered.

"I can't fight *him!*" Rick was barely able to whisper back. "He nearly killed the last guy he fought."

Tom understood now what Master Choso was up to, or thought he did. It was a joke. The master had never intended to take part in Tom's work. Tom was about to call things off when the decision was taken out of his hands. Wellington locked onto Rick like a hungry tiger sighting helpless prey.

"What are you waiting for, brat?" Wellington snapped. "You think you're so tough? Let's do it." His killer fist rocketed at Rick's face with crushing power, a crippling blow of such force and precision that nothing Tom could think of would be able to turn it aside.

**2**

To Tom's surprise, Master Choso's finger appeared between Wellington's fist and Rick's face, and with a graceful, almost imperceptible roll of a knuckle, he turned aside the blow so that it zipped harmlessly past Rick's ear.

Rick stood petrified, and Tom also found it difficult to move. The speed with which Wellington and Master Choso had moved, almost faster than Tom could follow, was breathtaking.

"Tomorrow, then?" Master Choso asked, as if nothing had happened.

"I think we'd better call it off," Tom said, but Rick shook his head.

"No, it's all right," he said. "I'll do it,

Tom." He glanced at Wellington, who looked amused. "It would be an honor."

Wellington sneered and turned away. Rick bowed to Master Choso, grabbed Tom by the arm, and dragged him from the martial arts school into the street.

"Are you crazy?" Tom shouted. "You're going to spar with that monster?" He could see in Rick's eyes the realization of what had almost happened, but then he saw Rick choke the panic back and harden it into determination.

"We'd better get to work," Rick said, "if I'm going to stand a chance in there."

The afternoon bell rang, and the students of Jefferson High scraped their books off their desks. They flooded the halls, racing for their lockers and homes.

At the stairwell Tom spotted Rick sitting on a step and staring woefully at nothing. "Hey, Rick," Tom said. But Rick didn't seem to notice he was there. "Rick!"

"Oh. Hi, genius." Rick took a deep breath. "Tom, I hope I'm ready."

Usually Rick was fearless, especially where sports were concerned. But despite Rick's determination, Tom knew he was terrified of getting into the ring with Duke Wellington.

"You don't have to fight him," Tom said. "I won't hold it against you if you don't."

"Don't be silly," Rick replied sullenly. "You've got an invention to test, and besides . . . Andrew Wellington." He spoke the name with a reverence that startled Tom. "That's the Duke's real name—Andrew. Started amateur karate at thirteen, was U.S. Armed Forces kickboxing champion before he started training with Master Choso and went professional. Four years later he defeated Master Choso for the world heavyweight title, just before the master retired. That was three years ago. No one's been able to touch him since. And he's had some pretty strong competition. Dangerous Danny DeVille, for instance."

"Dangerous Danny DeVille?" Tom repeated. He could barely keep from laughing.

"It's not funny!" Rick shouted. "It's like— it's like if you had a chance to have a conversation with Albert Einstein. Duke Wellington is the best. The best!"

"All the more reason for you not to fight someone with his training if you don't have to," Tom said.

"But I want to, Tom," Rick insisted. "How many other guys get to stand toe-to-toe with their idol? It's the opportunity of a lifetime. Besides," he continued, "Master Choso wouldn't let him go wild on me. We're not playing for keeps—it's just an exhibition."

"I guess you'll get through it okay," Tom said doubtfully.

"He's going to kill me, isn't he?" Rick said, but there was laughter in his voice.

Tom smiled back. "Not if I can help it."

"Hey, hey, if it isn't the kung fu fighter," came a voice from above them. Tom and Rick turned to see a young man with long, curly black hair walking down the stairs.

"Dan Coster!" said Tom. He had become friendly with Dan since moving to Central Hills, and through Dan he had met Dan's cousin, Mandy Coster.

"You know, Tom-Tom, the jock here"—Dan pointed at Rick—"is taking on some martial arts champion. That's the word, anyway. As soon as I heard about it, I just had to wish him luck."

Rick frowned. "How did you find out about that?"

"It's all over school," said Dan. "Say, if this is going to be a big bash, maybe you should get a rock and roll band to play, too. My group, the Scavengers, just happens to be free."

But neither Rick nor Tom was listening to him.

"How did word get out?" Rick wondered.

"Nobody knew about the match except Master Choso and us, and he wouldn't tell."

"I didn't say anything to anyone," Tom said.

Rick shook his head. "Me, neither. So who—?"

The answer hit them both at the same time. "Tina!"

Then they were both on the run, heading for the doors, leaving Dan Coster standing there.

"Hey!" Dan called after them. "So do you want the band or not?"

Tom and Rick burst through the exit and hit the schoolyard running. As they dashed through the yard, they glanced from side to side, scanning the faces of the students.

"There she is!" Rick shouted, whirling Tom around by the shoulder. He pointed to the parking lot, where a black-haired girl was leaning against a car, chatting with her friends. Tom had seen her before, but he didn't really know her.

Tina was Master Choso's sixteen-year-old daughter. Looking at her, no one would have guessed she had been in the country less than a year. Her clothes were totally American, and she spoke English better than most of Jefferson High's students.

Rick towered over her. "You overheard us, didn't you? Why'd you tell everyone I was sparring with Duke Wellington today? Now they'll all want to see my impression of a punching bag."

Tina's eyes flared. "You've got a lot of nerve, Rick Cantwell! Don't forget I live above that dojo, and my father says I can invite anyone there anytime I want."

"What's going on here?" said a nearby voice in sweet tones but with a harsh edge. Tom rolled his eyes as his younger sister, Sandra, placed herself between Rick and Tina. In the same class as Tina, Sandra dated Rick, and Rick winced to hear her disapproval.

"Back off, sis," Tom said as Rick stepped aside, embarrassed. "All we want to do is talk with Tina."

"If this is about your fight ..." Sandra began.

Tom glared at Tina. "I just want to know why you did it. This was supposed to be a quiet experiment. Now we'll be lucky if everyone in town doesn't show up."

"I think you're conceited and arrogant, Tom Swift, and I hope everyone in town does show up. Then they can see you fall flat on your face for once."

With that, she stormed off, leaving a puzzled Tom Swift scratching his head.

"I don't get it," he said. "What did I ever do to her?"

"For a smart guy, you sure can be dumb sometimes," Sandra replied with a sly smile. "I'd say she has a crush on you."

Tom stared at her as if she were crazy. "A crush? Don't mention that to Mandy, okay?" Mandy Coster was the girl Tom liked, and the last thing he needed in his life right now was girl trouble. He gazed for a long time at Tina, who was disappearing into the distance. "A crush, huh?"

By the time Tom and Rick reached Master Choso's dojo, the audience was spilling out into the street. "I know there's not much to do in this town," Rick said, "but this is ridiculous."

"It gets worse," said Tom. "Look!"

From the crowd emerged a dark-haired woman holding a microphone, followed by a man carrying videocamera equipment. Tom recognized her as Linda Nueve, a sportscaster for a TV station in Los Angeles.

"How did the media get wind of this?" Rick asked.

"There's the challenger," Ms. Nueve said

into her microphone as she made a beeline for Rick. "Mr. Cantwell, can we have a word with you?"

"No publicity," Tom whispered, tugging at Rick's sleeve. "This way."

They quickly skirted the edge of the crowd, slipping away from Ms. Nueve and her colleague. Just beyond the dojo they came to an alley and darted down it. At the back of the alley, next to a closed door, was parked a truck with the Swift Enterprises logo on it.

Tom hammered on the door of the truck. There was no answer. "My tech crew must be inside the dojo already," he said. He pulled at the back door to the dojo, but it was locked.

"Mr. Cantwell!" shouted Nueve from the far end of the alley. "Our viewers would like some questions answered. How were you chosen to fight the Duke? What's Swift Enterprises' connection to all this?"

"I wish she'd stop calling me Mr. Cantwell," Rick said to Tom. "It makes me feel like my father." He stood sullenly as Linda Nueve and her cameraman closed in.

Tom banged on the back door, and it finally swung open. "In here, guys," said a brusque, familiar voice. It was Harlan Ames, the security chief for Swift Enterprises. Tom and Rick dived past the older man, who quickly slammed the door behind them.

"I wondered why you wanted security on a thing like this," Harlan said.

"I needed someone I trusted to bring my equipment over," Tom replied, "and I don't want anyone getting in here."

"It's a little late for that," Harlan said, nodding toward the door to the next room.

A round little man with an ear-to-ear grin stood there in a suit that was slightly too small for him. He stepped forward, extending a hand to Tom and Rick. "Hi, there," the man said. "I'm Johnny Weisel." Rick shook the extended hand, and Weisel clamped his palm on Rick's bicep and squeezed. "Not bad but not world class. You'd better be able to give the humanoids a good show."

"Who are you?" Tom asked.

Weisel sneered at him, then glanced at Rick. "Who's *this* geek?" he said, waving a thumb in Tom's direction. "*I'm* Duke Wellington's manager."

"He's *my* manager," Rick replied. "And my friend."

Weisel guffawed. "Hey, friends won't get you anywhere in this game, kid." He tapped a fingertip on his forehead. "Brains and brawn are the ticket."

"We have to get ready," Tom said.

"Sure, sure," Weisel replied. He swaggered to the door, then stopped and looked back for a moment. "Nothing will get you ready enough for the Duke."

With one short burst of laughter, he was gone.

Tom whipped the canvas off a table that Harlan Ames had set up. On the table were what looked like several sheets of mesh, studded with black disks. Unfolded, they were revealed as a mesh shirt and tights. Beside them on the table was a laptop computer with a small black box attached to it by cables.

"Harlan has microcameras placed around the dojo so we can get input on Wellington's movements. I'll monitor you from this," Tom told Rick, setting a hand on the computer. "The black box is a special modem connected to the main computer back at the complex." He turned to Harlan. "Everything set with the satellite dish?"

"Hooked up in the van," Harlan answered. "Direct satellite connection to the complex."

"But we're only across town," Rick said, bewildered.

"We can't go through wires," said Tom. "Relay switches would slow us down. Satellite communication moves at the speed of light—and we need to be faster than the Duke."

As Rick peeled off his shirt, Tom pulled the cybernetic exoskeleton over Rick's head. Except for the black disks, which looked almost decorative, it was impossible to tell it from a simple fishnet T-shirt. A spasm rippled down Rick's arm. "How did that feel?" asked Tom.

"Not bad," Rick said. "Kind of invigorating, like you said." Rick then donned the disk-studded mesh tights, which fit like a second skin.

"That's an electrical discharge from the disk system locking into your nervous system," said Tom, attaching the other disks to Rick. "Remember, relax when you're out there. Try not to think about your movements, just get into the flow of things and let the cybersuit do the rest. We're training your body to react, not your mind."

"That's the first time I've ever heard you tell anyone not to think," Rick quipped. Then, suddenly he screamed as his body began to jerk uncontrollably. His arms flailed wildly, his legs twitched out from under him, and then he was on the floor, still writhing, an unconscious puppet on electronic strings.

**3**

HARLAN AMES DROPPED TO HIS KNEES AND tried to hold the jerking teenager still. Frantically Tom punched a key on the laptop, turning the system off. Then he pulled what looked like a penlight from his pocket and tore a disk away from the exoskeleton.

"I don't see what good a flashlight's going to do," Harlan said. Rick had stopped shaking when Tom cut the power, but he was still knocked out. Harlan rested him gently on the floor, tucking his jacket under Rick's head.

"It's not a flashlight, it's a little something I whipped up the other day," Tom said as he examined Rick. Rick's breathing and heart rate were both normal, and when he pried open Rick's eyes, Tom could see no signs of shock. He'd be all right. Tom turned his attention to the disk.

He held the "penlight" to it and pressed a switch. A soft hum came out instead of the light that Harlan Ames still expected. A second later the wafer-thin disk popped in two, revealing a vast array of microcircuits. Tom focused the pen over it. A second later he grinned, switched the "penlight" off, and snapped the disk casing shut.

"That's some tool you've got there," came a voice from behind him, and Tom turned, pleased to see Rick sitting up.

"It's a pocket-size infrasonics projector," Tom said, holding up the gizmo. "It puts out an adjustable, narrow pulse at frequencies much lower than our ears can hear. It's useful for all kinds of things, including making adjustments to the disks. How are you?"

Rick stretched. "Okay, I guess. What happened?"

"The system is still experimental. The disks are supposed to automatically adjust to changes in your system, but they don't always. I had this problem once before."

"You've done this before?" Rick asked.

"Oh!" said Tom, surprised. "Didn't I tell you about the robot?"

*     *     *

It was a week earlier that Tom Swift had finished work on the disks. He anxiously slipped on the fiber-optic exoskeleton and programmed his voice-activated computer with spoken commands. The tingling in his arms and legs thrilled him.

"Ballplayer," Tom said aloud.

A strip in the ceiling slid open, and a seventy-inch liquid crystal display television screen of Tom's design lowered. It flickered to life, and Tom saw on the screen a batter stepping up to the plate in some baseball game.

As the batter's hands gripped the bat and his arms curved back to wait for the oncoming baseball, Tom's hands also gripped an imaginary bat. At first he fought the sensation, then forced himself to relax. As if drawn by magnets, Tom's arms raised the phantom bat over his shoulder and locked in place. Tom decided it was an eerie feeling to surrender control of your muscles.

Suddenly his arms snapped forward, swinging the bat in a wide arc, and a jolt of impact ran from his wrists to his shoulders. He had hit an imaginary ball with his imaginary bat, sharing every sensation of the player on the screen. Then Tom's muscles were his own again, and he relaxed, excited by the experiment. His invention worked!

Now it was time for the next step.

"Kickboxer," Tom said, and the screen shimmered as the picture changed. A man stood there in a classic martial arts pose, frozen on the screen.

"Opponent," Tom ordered, and this time a mirrored wall panel slid up, revealing a man-shaped robot. As it moved, it slowly took on the more fluid motions of a human being until, by the time it faced Tom, it was able to bow, as one kickboxer on the screen was bowing to the other.

Tom returned the bow. Then, in a breathtaking second before he knew what was happening, Tom punched at the robot, his muscles once again under computer control. The robot barely deflected the blow, and Tom leapt high in the air as the robot fought back with a sweeping kick. Still in the air, his every move mimicking the fighters on the screen, Tom jabbed out with his heel, aiming for the area on the robot that on a man would have been the solar plexus.

A shock of pain ripped through Tom as flesh and blood smashed against unyielding metal. He dropped, barely maintaining a standing position as the fire exploding in his nerves ran into the impulses from the exoskeleton. Then it happened.

Like a man holding on to a live wire, Tom was aware of everything that was happening but unable to move. He tried to talk, to tell the computer to switch off the system, but even his mouth and tongue were frozen.

The system had locked up, more rigid than the robot had ever been.

The robot! It was advancing on him, feet kicking, arms throwing deadly punches. Tom made a mental note to add an emergency cutoff to its fight program—if he managed to get out of this alive.

The metal hands jabbed closer and closer. Though his limbs trembled with the effort, Tom was rooted to the spot. His mind raced for a solution while the robot moved in for the kill.

As a crushing steel limb plunged mindlessly at Tom with a force that could cave in his chest, the answer came to him. His body had locked in the robot's path. If effort did no good, he'd take the opposite tack and go limp.

His legs gave out, and he dropped and twisted under his own weight as the robot's crushing hand came down. It glanced off his shoulder, smashing the disk attached there. The circuit was broken, and Tom was free to move again. As the robot kicked and punched past him, he said "Off" through lips that were still stiff and tingling. The picture clicked off the screen, and the robot came to a standstill.

Tom took a deep breath and silently decided that working with a human being on the exoskeleton project might be a good idea.

"No, you didn't mention the robot," Rick said. "That's not going to happen today, is it?"

"Not a chance," Tom said, adjusting the last disk on the exoskeleton. "I realized that the system was set for me. Obviously, it has to be adjusted for each wearer's biochemistry. It should work fine now."

Rick just shook his head and put on a head guard, strapping it under his chin. He pulled on special foam-filled vinyl gloves, and on his feet went open-bottomed high-topped boots that protected his ankles while letting the soles of his feet touch the floor. Finally he pulled on a loose white jacket and pants and tightened a sash around the waist.

"You look like a real warrior," Tom said. "Let's go get him."

Side by side they walked out into the dojo's main room, where a boxing ring was set up. Though the room was small, built to accommodate a class of normally no more than twenty, today it was packed with a horde of cheering people, each struggling to get a good view of the ring. Tom recognized many of his classmates. Near the entrance, pressed against the front window, Linda Nueve fumed, her cameraman struggling for a view of the ring.

Seated in the front row, near a worried Sandra, was a man Tom had never seen before: a lean, dark-eyed man with a goatee. His dark red hair had been shaved into a widow's peak that looked like an arrow pointing to his hawklike nose.

In the ring was Duke Wellington. If Wellington had looked monstrous before, now, dressed in a bodysuit that highlighted his massive muscles, he looked like an unstoppable engine of destruction. As Rick entered the ring, Wellington bared his teeth in a frightening snarl.

"Remember, Rick. Relax," Tom warned. Then he slipped out of the room and back to his computer.

By the time Tom had settled in his chair and switched on his equipment, the preliminaries were over. He watched on his TV monitor as Master Choso stepped from the ring. Rick and the Duke stood face-to-face in the center of the ring and bowed ceremoniously to each other, Wellington never taking his eyes off his opponent. Watching the screen, Tom saw Wellington's lips move, and the computer read his lips and translated the motion into words:

"Go a couple of rounds and then fall down, kid. I'll try to take it easy on you."

They backed off, dancing around each other. The Duke made a couple of faint swipes. Rick backstepped away.

"Okay," Tom said. "Here goes." He tapped a couple of keys on the computer.

Rick moved in quickly, ducking under Wellington's massive arms and planting two punches on the Duke's jaw. Wellington, stunned more than hurt, staggered back a step, and Rick spun a side thrust kick into Wellington's chest. The champ went back off his feet.

"It works!" Tom shouted. Up until that second he hadn't been sure. But the computer had read Wellington's movements and shifted Rick to good striking position.

"If that's how you want to play it, kid," said Tom's computer as it mimicked Wellington's words. Rick backed up, shifting to defensive position, his arms crossed in front of him.

BLIP!

"No!" Tom shouted, but he knew Rick couldn't hear him. Another blip jumped onto Tom's computer screen. Rick was tensing into his favorite karate move, in contrast to what the computer was telling his muscles to do. "Get into the flow, Rick! Don't go against it!"

It was too late. Tom watched helplessly as Rick leapt in, swiping the stiffened edge of his hand at the pressure points in Wellington's arm.

Effortlessly the Duke elbowed Rick's punch aside. A roundhouse right crashed into Rick's face, and he dropped to the mat like a stone.

**4**

**I**'M SORRY," CAME A TIMID VOICE FROM BEHIND Tom.

He spun in his chair to see Tina standing there, tearful eyes on the monitor where her father stood over Rick, slowly counting to ten.

"I didn't mean any of those things I said," she continued. "I just wanted ... I was just so angry ... I'm so sorry...."

"It's not over yet," Tom said. His fingers flew over the computer keyboard.

"Six," came Master Choso's words from the computer.

"There's nothing anyone can do," Tina said.

"Seven," the computer blurted.

"I'm not just anyone. I've already done it," Tom replied.

"Eight."

On the TV screen Rick's whole body convulsed. His eyes snapped open.

"Nine."

"Come on, Rick, come on!" Tom heard his sister shout.

Rick pressed himself up from the mat just before the ten-count. The crowd went wild. Rick wobbled on his feet and brushed at his eyes as if trying to wipe away mental cobwebs. His back was turned to the monster angrily storming at him.

Suddenly Master Choso was between Wellington and his target. "Wait until he is ready," the master snapped. Wellington froze. For a long moment they faced off, then Wellington backed away.

Rick steadied himself and lifted his hands in front of his face, ready to continue the fight. The audience let loose another roar.

"How did you do that?" asked Tina, amazed. "He was way gone."

"Simple," said Tom. "I overloaded the disks he's wearing. Sort of like when a surgeon slaps electric paddles on the chest of a dying patient to start his heart. The trick was to let the disks overload enough to give him a shock he'd feel, without putting so much juice through them that they'd burn out."

"Maybe it wasn't such a good idea," Tina said. "Look!"

Master Choso had stepped out of the way, and Wellington charged at Rick again. Rick stood lead footed, an easy target for the huge champion. Wellington slammed a sweeping kick at Rick.

By reflex Rick dropped under the kick. It whizzed harmlessly over his head.

"Great!" Tom shouted. By the readings on the computer screen, he saw the disks were in control. "Rick's moving instinctively, defensively. As long as he lets the disks direct him, he doesn't have a thing to worry about."

Even as Tom spoke, his eyes widened. On the screen Wellington planted a jab on Rick's jaw, a blow only slightly deflected by Rick's face guard. Then another and another. Rick staggered back, stumbling against the ropes.

Duke Wellington moved in for the kill.

Just before the Duke's mighty fists rained down, Rick dropped to the mat. His legs slid around Wellington's foot. Rick whipped himself over abruptly, knocking Wellington's leg out from under him. The champ toppled backward.

Before Wellington's shoulders hit the mat,

he hurled his hands back, using them to cushion the fall. The fall turned into a backward roll and the backward roll into a handspring. Before Tom knew it the Duke was on his feet again, to the appreciative applause of the audience.

Even Tom had to admire the move. "That's exactly what I mean," he excitedly told Tina. "He didn't think about that maneuver. He didn't have time to. He just did it." Tom patted his computer affectionately. "And now it's part of my data base, for the use of anyone who has the potential skill to do it."

"I thought your disks would let Rick do anything," Tina said.

Tom shook his head. "I can't work miracles. The disks wouldn't help someone who's completely out of shape. His body just wouldn't have the necessary reactions. But someone like Rick, who's limber and athletic, has all the capabilities. All he needs is knowledge."

"And in a hurry!" cried Tina, pointing at the screen, her face suddenly ashen.

Watching the monitor, they saw Rick floundering, with only the ropes keeping him on his feet. A punch smashed into his chest, knocking the wind out of him. Wellington lifted up Rick's chin with his left hand, and very slowly brought his right fist all the way back, taking careful aim.

Then the bell rang, signaling the end of the round.

Tom sprang from his seat and rushed to ringside. Rick straddled the ropes in his corner, catching his breath and gulping water from a plastic jug.

"Pretty good so far, huh?" Rick quipped when he saw Tom.

"You're getting killed," Tom replied, and he wasn't laughing. "I can't let you go out there again."

"Aw, you're turning into an old lady," Rick said. "It's only an exhibition. I'll be all right. I'll be done in five or six minutes."

"Sorry, pal. You've been out there only five minutes."

As Tom's words sank in, Rick looked sick. "That means . . ."

Tom nodded. "You have another three rounds to get through, at least. We could throw in the towel, you know."

Rick snarled at the thought. "I might be black and blue, but I'm no quitter. Looks like you're back to the drawing board with your disks, though."

"There's nothing wrong with them," Tom said curtly, and instantly wished he hadn't.

Rick was right. The system simply wasn't working well enough. "It's you," he continued. "It's not that you're not good enough. You're *too* good. You're resisting the disks, trying to do it on your own. It's a bad combination. Maybe we should just quit before you get really hurt."

"Not on your life," Rick snapped. "You let *me* fight the fight!" He spritzed what was left of the water into his face and shook the liquid from his hair. "Get back to your station, genius. We've got us a match to win."

Tom smiled feebly, taken aback by Rick's behavior. It was unlike Rick to dismiss Tom that lightly, and it displayed a new arrogance that could only mean trouble. Rick might pass for a star on the high-school gridiron, but in the Duke's world he was dangerously outmatched—unless Tom got the cybersuit working perfectly.

He went over the system in his head, checking his figures. "There's no reason it shouldn't work," he muttered. He glanced at his watch. Thirty seconds until the next round. Tom hurried toward the back room, anxious to do everything he could to keep Rick safe.

As he approached the door, Harlan Ames came through it, shoving before him a trembling Johnny Weisel. "I found him monkeying around with your computer," Harlan said.

Tom's eyes flared with anger, and Weisel threw his arms in front of his face as if afraid Tom would hit him. "I didn't do anything!" Weisel shouted, too quickly to be telling the truth. "I like video games, it looked like a video game, you got video games on that thing, don't you, kid?" He forced a sick smile that made Tom even angrier.

"What are you doing to my manager!" roared a husky voice from the ring. Before anyone knew what was happening, Duke Wellington charged from the ring and grabbed Weisel from Ames's grip. Weisel scurried behind Wellington for safety. "Think you're tough, old man?" Wellington challenged.

Tom didn't like the look on Harlan's face. The security chief wasn't exactly young, but he was as tough as ever and backed down to no one. Harlan was just starting to speak when Tom stepped between him and Wellington.

"Weisel was trying to foul up my experiment," Tom said.

"Listen!" Wellington shouted. His powerful fingers locked onto Tom's collar, squeezing it tight around Tom's neck. "You call my manager a cheat, you're calling *me* a cheat! You calling me a cheat, punk?"

The bell rang. "Contestants, return to the ring," Master Choso ordered. "If Duke Wellington is not in the ring in fifteen seconds, the round will be awarded to Rick Cantwell."

"Later for you, kid. I've got to put your pal out of his misery first." Effortlessly the Duke shoved Tom back, ramming him into Harlan with such force that both were knocked off their feet.

"We ought to make a citizen's arrest and turn those two menaces over to the cops," Harlan muttered as he picked himself up.

"Forget it," Tom said. "I've got a better way to deal with him." As Wellington climbed into the ring with seconds to go, Tom scurried into the back room and sat before his computer.

"Oh, no," he moaned.

The screen was blank. Somehow Weisel had shut everything down. Then a shadow moved beside Tom on the wall, and he laughed despite himself. It was one of the rare moments he felt totally stupid. Tina Choso stooped to plug the equipment back into the wall.

"Thanks," Tom said as his screens flared to life. His fingers raced over the computer keyboard. "Now we'll show them."

Rick danced backward around the ring, staying out of Wellington's grasp. The big man swung. Rick ducked. Wellington kicked, and Rick jumped to one side.

Tom finished his equipment check. "Keep your fingers crossed," he said, even though he knew Rick couldn't hear him. "All systems go."

Wellington forced Rick into a corner and then backed away so that Rick could come out. As Rick moved, the Duke clipped him across the chest with a hard chop, then another, then another. Rick fell back, gasping for air.

As he dropped, he went into a backward roll–handspring combination that brought him to his feet. It was a perfect mirror image of the maneuver Wellington had pulled off in the previous round. Bounding to his feet, Rick bounced back into the ropes and slingshot off them, hurling himself into Wellington.

Even the champ was caught off guard. Rick twisted in midair, jarring his elbow back into Wellington's solar plexus. Rick's feet touched the mat, and he spun, smacking a backhand against the Duke's ear. Wellington swayed on his feet.

At ringside Weisel went white as a sheet.

Then Rick made an inside high-kick, planting all his force against Wellington's chin. The champ's eyes went glassy. His knees wobbled. He crashed to the mat and didn't move.

The sheer speed of it had taken Tom's breath away. From somewhere he could hear a frantic Johnny Weisel screaming, "Get up! Get up!" Rick looked smug as Master Choso counted to ten and raised Rick's hand in the air.

Then, as the crowd shrieked and rushed the ring, a realization struck Tom like a bolt of lightning.

Rick had just beaten the heavyweight kickboxing champion of the world!

**5**

"LAST NIGHT, CENTRAL HILLS RESIDENTS CELE-brated when a local boy, still in high school, took on one of the monsters of the martial arts world and won," Linda Nueve reported on the TV news.

Tom switched off the sound in disgust. He and Rick were sitting in the den of the Swift house. "I didn't want any publicity. One of the reasons I decided to try out the disks with kickboxing was that not too many people follow the sport yet."

"They do now, thanks to her," Rick said, nodding at the screen.

The camera moved in on the Swift Enter-prises van that had been parked in the alleyway. Tom groaned. Then a ranch-style house flashed on the screen.

"That's my house!" Rick blurted. "Turn it up."

Tom hit a button on the remote control, and the sound was on again. ". . . is not where you would expect to find talent of the caliber necessary to beat world heavyweight champions."

"What does she mean by that?" said Rick, outraged.

"Shh," Tom replied as Master Choso's stern face came onto the screen. "I want to hear this."

"This was not a championship bout," Master Choso said in calm tones. "We were asked by Swift Enterprises to help test a new invention. My friend Andrew Wellington was kind enough to lend his considerable expertise to the project. The outcome does not affect his professional standing in any way."

As Linda Nueve's voice sounded, the scene changed again. "Others were not treating the match so lightly."

Johnny Weisel's round face, reddened with rage, huffed into view. "Nobody humiliates us! Nobody! Especially not some high-school punk from Nowheresville! It was a set-up job, but we're ready now. We know all about you, punk, you and your fancy pals and fancy electronics. You're too chicken to meet us for a rematch because next time the Duke will knock your block off!"

Then Nueve was back on the screen, speaking intently into her microphone. "That was Wellington's manager, Johnny Weisel, speaking for the champion, who was not available for comment. Nor has there been any comment from Richard Cantwell or Swift Enterprises on the incident. Reporting from Central Hills, this is Linda Nueve."

Tom clicked off the set, strolled over to the window, and looked out toward the front gates of the complex. Beyond the front gates news trucks still sat, waiting for a glimpse of Tom or Rick.

"What did your dad say when he heard?" Rick asked.

Tom winced when he thought about the phone call he had received that morning from Washington, D.C., where Tom senior was holding meetings with NASA. It was one of the few times his father had ever been short with him. "He's not happy. He wants me to resolve this thing as quickly as possible. Swift Enterprises is involved in a lot of classified research, and all this publicity is getting in the way."

"How does he expect you to stop it?" said Rick.

Tom thought about that for a moment. "I suppose we could just let Duke Wellington pound you into a pulp and hope everyone loses interest."

Rick puffed up, looking ready for action. "Bring him on. I tell you, Tom, I feel great! I could take him on again and again."

"So you told me last night when the match ended," said Tom. "That's something else I wanted to talk about. Come on, I want to check you out."

Tom snapped his fingers. A section of wall slid up in the den, revealing a secret corridor into the technical complex. Cool blue light guided them along the pure white passageway as the panel slid closed behind them.

"What's to check?" Rick asked.

"I just want to make sure you're okay. We're messing around with the nervous system and the body's metabolism. By all my calculations it should be quite safe. But it never hurts to double-check."

"Says you," Rick replied curtly. "I feel great, maybe better than I've ever felt in my life. Isn't that good enough for you?"

Tom didn't respond. If something in his

friend *was* different, he wasn't sure it was for the better.

They entered Tom's private laboratory, which was filled with equipment that Rick had never seen before. "I borrowed these from the medical technologies division," Tom explained. "I made a few adjustments of my own, of course. They'll be able to give us a complete physical readout."

"You going to jab me or poke me or anything like that?" Rick asked.

Tom chuckled. "Some fighter you are. No. See that screen over there? All you have to do is stand behind it. It all works on infrasonics, on the same basic principle as a CAT scan." Rick took his place behind the screen, and his silhouette appeared on it. "Basically, it makes a duplicate image of you on computer, and we can see in the duplicate any abnormalities. . . . Hmm, that's odd. . . ."

"What's wrong?" Rick asked anxiously.

"Hmmm?" Tom was so focused on the screen that he had hardly heard his friend. "Oh. Nothing. Nothing to worry about, anyway. You're in perfect shape."

"Perfect?" Rick said. "People don't look as concerned as you do over 'perfect.' "

"That's the problem," said Tom. "You're too perfect." He ran a finger along the image of Rick's arm. "Here and in other places, the muscles should be stretched and stressed. You never used them before in the way you used them yesterday. But they're not only in fine condition, there's more muscle mass than the last time I checked you. Of course, this is better equipment, but still . . ."

"So stop fussing, Tom." Rick, all grins, stepped from behind the screen. "I tell you, I've never been better." He took two playful swings at Tom, who batted them away.

"That's another thing—" Tom began, but an intercom buzzer interrupted him. He switched on the wall unit, and a picture resolved on the viewscreen.

It was Harlan Ames. Tom could see this was a business call, not a friendly one. "Tom! Thank heavens, I found you."

"What's the matter, Harlan?"

"It's those news crews," Harlan said. "They're getting in the way of everyone coming in and leaving. I called Chief Montague down at police headquarters, but she said as long as they're parked on the street and they aren't coming onto Swift property, there's nothing the police can do about it except maybe give out some parking tickets. But we can't have them out there photographing everyone who passes through the gates—we'll lose our security rating."

"I know, I know," Tom said. "Dad told me the same thing. But what can I do? Destroy my invention and tell them it's all over?"

"No!" shouted Rick, a bit too emphatically for Tom's tastes. He made a mental note to keep an eye on Rick's behavior.

Across the road from Swift Enterprises, Linda Nueve sipped a bottle of mineral water and stared out the window of her van. She rubbed her eyes. She had kept her vigil outside the complex since the night before, breaking only for short naps, but she was no closer to getting her story, and now half the television stations in Los Angeles had sportscasters up here, too.

Bored, she fast-forwarded through the videotapes that played on every monitor in the small van. They were tapes of everyone who had been to Swift Enterprises that morning. Men and women, short, tall, fat, slender. Then her eyes fell on an almost familiar face. The man, wearing dark glasses and a hat that was part of the uniform of someone who stocked vending machines for a living, seemed oddly furtive as he glanced around on his way into the complex.

She froze the shot for her cameraman to see. "Don't we know this guy from somewhere?"

The cameraman mulled it over. "Yeah, it's ... uh ... you know, it's whatsisname, the other guy."

"You're a big help."

"You know. Him. The guy at the fight last night."

Her eyes widened. "Him! What's he doing. . . ?" Frantically she zipped through videotape after videotape. "Where's the shot of him coming out?"

"That's all the footage we took. That's everyone."

"Then he's still—" She stopped, her ears pricking up. "What's that noise?"

It began as a soft whir, like a distant fan. Then the beating grew louder and louder, until she could hear nothing else.

"Helicopter!" Linda Nueve shouted over the racket, and she barreled out of the van. Overhead she saw the black craft swoop, emblazoned with the Swift Enterprises logo.

Tom Swift leaned out of it and waved, grinning.

"It's that other kid, the inventor. They're both in there." Angrily she ran to the front of the van and climbed in behind the wheel.

Already the other news vans were forming a caravan in pursuit of the chopper. Still, she sensed something wasn't right. She could smell a story, something everyone else was overlooking, and she was going to get it. And no kid, not even Tom Swift, was going to stop her.

"Ha!" shouted Tom as he gazed down on the line rolling along the streets beneath the chopper. "That'll get them off our back."

"Since we can't go back to the complex, mind telling me where we're going to land?" Rick asked.

"We've got fuel, don't we?" Tom asked the pilot, who didn't turn his helmeted head but nodded silently in reply. "Let's run them around awhile. That'll give us time to figure out what to do next."

To the pilot he said, "Keep low and stay along the road. We want them following us for as long as possible. And radio the complex to let them know everything's going according to plan."

"Some plan," said Rick.

To Tom's surprise, the helicopter started rising. They swerved north, heading over the mountains above Central Hills.

"Hey!" Tom shouted. "Didn't you hear me?"

Again the pilot nodded, but the copter kept rising. The pilot lifted the transceiver from the radio. With a yank, he tore the cord loose. They were now isolated from the rest of the world.

"I want the exoskeleton," the pilot said in a cold, deliberate voice. He pulled off his helmet and turned around.

Tom knew that face. He had seen it at the match: the man in front, with his red hair shaped like an arrow—a mystery man who now held the controls of the helicopter, and their lives, in his hands.

**6**

"DANGEROUS DANNY DEVILLE!" GASPED RICK.

"The key word is *dangerous*," DeVille replied. "You're going to give me what it takes to beat Duke Wellington—"

Before Tom or Rick could react, DeVille threw the transceiver out his vent window.

"Or you'll follow that down—and it's a long way down."

"Who is this guy?" Tom asked, keeping his voice even.

"Arrgh!" DeVille screamed at the top of his lungs. "I can't believe you've never heard of me! Everyone's heard of me!"

"A lot of people haven't even heard of kick-boxing," Tom pointed out.

"Kid, don't tick me off." With that, DeVille shoved the helicopter into a nosedive.

Tom sat silently and swallowed hard as the helicopter plunged toward the ground. Rick, oddly, cowered where he sat, his eyes locked on Tom. It wasn't at all like Rick in the face of danger, and Tom wondered what was going on.

DeVille howled wildly as the ground rushed up to greet them. They were on the high ridge of the mountains, with nothing below them but craggy peaks.

"Think you got guts, kid?" DeVille yelled as a rocky death loomed ever closer.

He won't kill himself, Tom thought. He's not that crazy.

Tom stared out the window at the jagged crag that rushed at him. It was suddenly gone, replaced by clear blue sky as the helicopter leveled and soared scant feet above the rocky ground.

"Did you like that, kid?" said DeVille through mocking laughter. "Like I said, *dangerous*."

"That was pretty good, the way you got us away on this helicopter," Tom said, playing to the big man's ego. "How'd you manage to get past the security at Swift Enterprises? Only the best could pull that off."

DeVille pondered the question. "I *am* the best. Got in disguised as service personnel, then I hid out until you showed your faces. Once I got wind of what you were up to, it was a cinch to knock out your pilot and take his place. I was a chopper pilot in the service," he said, turning around to show them his evil grin.

Tom saw his opening. "Rick!" he shouted. "Now!"

Tom dived across DeVille to grab the control stick. It was too late. DeVille slammed an elbow into Tom's ribs. Through a red haze of pain, Tom dimly saw the ground ahead. The helicopter was flying parallel to it, skimming the tops of trees.

"Rick!" he yelled again. He heard something crack. It was the landing guides, smacking the treetops.

Then Rick lunged at DeVille, grabbing him across the face while wrapping an arm around his neck, and pulling him back off Tom. DeVille had a viselike grip on the copter's joystick. When Rick yanked him back, the stick came free and the craft began to spin out of control.

Tom opened the side bay door of the helicopter. "Jump!" he shouted at Rick.

"What?" Rick glanced out the door. There was nothing below them but trees.

"Jump!" Tom repeated. The helicopter lurched and rolled, and a surprised DeVille fell out of the chopper.

"Is he—?" Rick began as Tom scrambled to the remaining helicopter controls.

"I don't know," Tom said, "but *we* will be in a few seconds if we don't get out of here. This helicopter's completely out of control. We have to jump."

"You're kidding!" Rick said. "What about parachutes?"

Tom shook his head. "We're too low to the ground. They wouldn't open in time."

As the helicopter brushed the boughs of a tree, Rick and Tom hurled themselves out. Tom crashed through the tree, flailing as pine needles scratched him. His fingers grazed bark and tightened in desperation. He felt the muscles in his arms stretch beyond endurance, but he held on. In a burst of relief he realized his fall was broken.

"Rick!" he yelled, fearing the worst. Nothing.

Then a voice came from somewhere below. "Tom? What are you still doing up there? Can't keep up with the real men?"

It was Rick! He had survived.

As Tom climbed down to the ground, an explosion rocked the hillside. It was the helicopter, crashing in the distance. Tom looked around.

"Any idea where we are?" Rick asked.

Tom nodded. "Somewhere up in the mountains. Central Hills is due south. It can't be too far."

"If we get there before dark." Rick looked at the sinking sun. "It gets pretty cold up here at night. Ever create a fire?"

"I don't know," Tom said. "I really hate stealing other people's inventions."

Rick laughed. "Then we'd better get walking."

"I'm getting a bit worried about you," Tom confided as they moved down the hill. The wind was picking up, and he felt the evening chill.

"Why?" Rick asked. He was back to his old confident, cheery self.

"I'm worried about your mood changes," Tom said. "After all, we've been tampering with your neurosystem. Who knows what kind of reactions the disks triggered?"

Rick shrugged. "I feel better than ever. You checked me out yourself, remember? You said I was in perfect shape."

"Too perfect. You should be in *worse* shape

than you are. Your responses are getting strange, too. There are moments when you've gotten extremely reckless, but you actually seemed petrified up there in the helicopter."

Rick cleared aside some brush so they could pass. "I didn't know how far I could go up there. I figured it was better to let you do the thinking. Hey, it was your helicopter."

The explanation sounded too pat to Tom, but he let it go. He didn't care about explanations, he wanted to know how Rick would act next.

"What if I said I didn't want you using the disks anymore?" Tom said.

Rick blanched. "You're kidding."

"I said, what if?" Tom studied his friend carefully. A look of panic had flashed across Rick's face, to be replaced by a relaxed calm when Tom had spoken again.

"That would be okay, I guess," Rick replied, after considerable thought. "It would be too bad, though. Like I said, it's a great invention."

"How does it feel when you're wearing the cybersuit?" Tom asked when they had gone a little farther.

"Great," Rick said. A warm glow of memory seeped across his face, a look that made

Tom uncomfortable. "You did a great job on it. I barely knew it was there."

Maybe his expression means nothing, Tom told himself. Maybe I'm making too much out of this. But he couldn't shake his uneasiness. He felt he had opened a doorway to trouble, and Rick was his unintended victim.

"I don't mean that," Tom said. "How do *you* feel when you're wearing the suit? What sensations do you have?"

"Great," Rick repeated. "I knew I was fighting the system at first. I guess deep down inside I didn't want to hand myself over to a machine. That was the biggest mistake I ever made."

"Why do you say that?"

"Why?" said Rick. "You've worn the disks! You have to ask that? Man, those things are sheer power. When they kick in, you feel like you're being charged and charged and charged. You feel like you can do anything."

"Like take on somebody twice your size?"

Rick smiled. "Yeah. Like that."

Tom pressed on, aware that darkness was closing in around them. "Can you tell me when you first got this sensation of power?"

Rick thought about it for a moment. "I'm not really sure. Maybe—"

"Who cares?" said a nearby voice, cutting him off.

"It can't be," said Rick.

"It is," Tom said as a shiver ran through him.

They spun around to find themselves facing an irate Dangerous Danny DeVille. "The power," DeVille continued, "that's the important part. I want that power."

Tom's eyes darted about as the red-haired man moved slowly toward them. There were trees all around and no easy path for escape. Tom's heart sank. If DeVille was as good as Rick claimed he was, there was no way they could beat him. Not without the exoskeleton, and that was far, far away.

"Here and now, punk," DeVille said, furious eyes fixed on Tom. "Let's finish it."

Tom shifted to a defensive stance, his arms half lowered, his legs spread to balance his weight as comfortably as the sloping terrain would allow. "Aren't you forgetting something?" he asked. "I'm the only one who can get you the disks and who knows how the system works. Hurt me, and you end up with nothing."

DeVille smirked and moved closer. "How about I rip your face off, wear it as a mask, and walk into your complex and take everything I want?"

Rick stepped between them. "Leave him to me, Tom. I can take him."

DeVille cocked an eye. "I was going to get to you, punk, but if you want to go first, I can get into that."

He curled his fingers and jabbed the heel of his hand at Rick's head, in a move called a tiger's claw. But the loose ground gave way as DeVille shifted his weight, and his foot slid downhill, throwing him off balance. Rick dodged the tiger's claw, but DeVille adjusted his stance and threw another punch with lightning speed. The blow clipped the side of Rick's head, just above the ear.

"That's just for openers," DeVille said as Rick stumbled back. "Where's that power you were boasting about?"

He charged Rick. To Tom's surprise, Rick didn't back away but instead moved forward. DeVille punched out on the run, but Rick slid outside the punch, delivering an uppercut to DeVille's ribs and sliding his hand up under DeVille's arm. In a flash his fingers locked around DeVille's shoulder and his leg wrapped behind DeVille's knee. Rick pushed.

DeVille toppled backward, smashing into the dirt. His foot shot up, the hard toe of his shoe poking Rick in the shoulder. Rick screamed, his arm dangling uselessly at his side.

"Pressure points," sneered DeVille as he got to his feet. "If there's anything left of you when I get finished, learn to use them. Wellington never did."

"Yeah," Rick replied. "And he's only the heavyweight champion of the world."

As Rick bent slightly, nursing his arm, DeVille leapt high in the air, spinning as he jumped. His heel cracked across Rick's jaw. Rick fell, unconscious.

DeVille landed deftly, nudging Rick with his toe. Rick didn't move. It was over almost before Tom could react. DeVille turned toward Tom and wagged his finger, motioning Tom to step forward.

"Just one thing," said Tom. "If you're so much better, why is Wellington the champion?"

"You really get on my nerves, kid," DeVille said. His voice was little more than a whispered rumble that sent chills through Tom. "Now you get to feel why Dangerous Danny DeVille rules the world!"

DeVille let out a startling shriek. Before Tom could move, DeVille's heel crashed against his chest. Off his feet Tom rolled down a ravine and lay there in a pile of fallen leaves and branches, staring up, dazed, at the smirking figure hovering above him.

I've got the skills to fight, Tom realized suddenly. I wore the disks, I took the training. I must've learned *something* from that.

With another shout DeVille hurled himself off the lip of the ravine, driving his feet down at Tom's midsection. A second before impact Tom rolled out of the way. DeVille slipped in leaves loosely scattered on the ground. On his knees Tom jabbed at DeVille with a knife hand, his fingers straight and rigid, held tightly together.

DeVille threw a fist, knocking Tom aside. Crouching warily, they circled for what seemed to Tom an incredibly long time. He knew fear was altering his perceptions and that he faced a man far more powerful and skilled than he was. He choked back the fear and focused.

As if controlled by the same mind, they attacked at the same instant, with flying kicks that snapped out in midair. Both deflected the other's kick, and they landed opposite each other, spinning as their feet touched ground to face off, crouched and ready for the next action.

Do the unexpected, Tom told himself.

He ran, clawing and kicking his way up the side of the ravine. In a flash he was at the top and scrambling through the brush there, trying to find enough darkness to hide in.

DeVille was after him like a shot. Tom knew DeVille thought he had given up, but that was what Tom wanted him to think. It was time to take the fight off DeVille's terms.

He breathed harder than he needed to, hoping DeVille would think he was winded. Tom paused, pressing his back against a tree. He listened carefully. Where was DeVille?

"Looking for someone?" came DeVille's cold voice, booming now. Tom snapped his head around. He saw nothing. "You really don't want to live very long, do you, kid?" said DeVille. Tom glanced up, and his eyes widened in shock. Somehow DeVille had gotten into the tree above him.

DeVille dropped softly to the ground. Taking position with one fist extended and the other turned up and drawn in under his arm, DeVille smiled a killer's smile. Then the extended fist jerked back and the upturned one shot forward.

Tom sucked in a hard breath and dived to one side. DeVille's fist smacked into the tree. To Tom's surprise, DeVille seemed unaffected. Tom looked closer and gasped.

DeVille had stopped his blow a fraction of an inch from the tree. Laughing, DeVille said, "You didn't expect to get me with that old ploy, did you? I heard you were a smart kid, but I guess you never heard of muscle control, sitting in your laboratory all day."

He swung a roundhouse kick at Tom. Tom barely knocked it aside with his hand and stepped back, but DeVille followed with another roundhouse and another, spinning his whole body around for full sweeps. Another kick caught Tom on his left shoulder, as Rick had been caught, and Tom's arm went limp.

"Pressure points, kid."

Tom stumbled back, his arm useless at his side. The disk training was keeping him in the fight, but nothing could have prepared him for the mad fighter pressing him. With the full setup and computer link, he might have stood a chance, he knew, but now, relying on his memory . . .

A kick caught him in the stomach, and the breath exploded from him. He twisted and fell, clutching at a large, smooth boulder. The kickboxer was right above him, sizing him up. "End of the line, kid," DeVille said. "Don't worry, it'll be fun—for *me!*"

**7**

TOM FLOPPED HELPLESSLY, GASPING FOR breath as DeVille took careful aim. "You could have saved yourself a lot of trouble if you had just given me those disks, kid."

"Forget it," Tom mumbled. "I'll never help you."

DeVille shook his head. "You don't need all those ribs, do you?"

He leapt into the air and flexed his leg back into a flying knee drop. The knee plunged toward a crushing impact in Tom's side. Concentrating, unflinching, Tom watched it fall.

At the last possible instant he rolled aside. DeVille's eyes flared with surprise and anger, but there was no time for him to shift his body. His unprotected knee struck the boulder with a violent crunch.

DeVille screamed. His face twisted with pain as he clutched his knee and toppled next to Tom. For a long time they lay there on the ground, Tom catching his breath, DeVille howling and nursing his knee.

The cool air stung Tom's face, and suddenly he remembered Rick. Somewhere in the dark, his friend was unconscious. He scrambled down the ravine to search for him.

"You can't leave me!" DeVille cried. "I can't survive out here by myself, not with a broken leg."

"If you've got a broken leg, I'll need help to move you or it will just make things worse," Tom replied. "If Rick isn't too injured to lend a hand, we'll be right back."

"And if he is?" DeVille whined.

Tom shook his head. "You should have thought of that before you decided to beat us up."

Tom found Rick among the trees in the ravine as the last light faded. His friend groaned as Tom helped him to his feet.

"Wake up, sleepyhead," Tom joked. "You missed all the action."

"Hey, a guy's got to get naps in where he

can," Rick quipped back, and Tom knew he was all right. Rick looked around, bewildered. "What happened to the Dangerous One?"

Grinning, Tom blew on his knuckles and brushed them against his shirt. "He's out of the way for the moment. I took care of him."

"You?" Rick said, astonished. "You took him and I couldn't? I must be losing my touch. Say, is it my imagination or is it getting chilly out here?"

"You got it," said Tom. "I don't think we'll be getting out of here tonight."

"Looks like you'll have to use someone else's invention after all," Rick said.

DeVille howled all the way back to the ravine, where Tom cleared away leaves and wood, then dug a shallow pit with a stone while Rick searched for small boulders. They set them in a circle around the pit and tossed in the leaves and branches.

"Be careful," Tom said. "We've got to keep the flames contained. We don't want to start a forest fire."

"That's if we get any flames," Rick answered. With a small stone he put a point on a stick and ground the pointed end into a flat piece of bark. He rubbed the stick between his hands, spinning it rapidly. "I know the trick is to build up friction until you get enough heat, but it doesn't seem to be working."

"Why do it the hard way?" asked Tom.

"I suppose you brought matches," Rick said.

"No," replied Tom. "Better." He popped his infrasonic pen from his pocket and began to calibrate the instrument.

"How is sound going to help us?" asked Rick. "We need a campfire, not a rock concert."

"Hold the stick against the bark," Tom said, "and watch."

Rick did as Tom asked, and Tom carefully aimed the nose of the infrasonic pen at the pointed end of the stick. The stick shuddered in Rick's hands, but he held it down, as still as possible.

Smoke wafted from the bark, and then came a burst of sparks. They had fire!

Quickly Rick dropped to his hands and knees and blew softly, then harder on the sparks. A small fire flared up and quickly spread across the pit.

"The pen emits sonic vibrations," Tom explained. "They 'rubbed' the stick on the bark harder and faster than our hands could."

"In other words," Rick said, "instant friction." He motioned with his thumb over his shoulder at DeVille, who was curled up on the ground, still groaning and clutching his knee. "What about him?"

Making sure not to let DeVille's injured leg touch the ground, they dragged him to the fire the same way they had moved him down the ravine. Despite threats from DeVille, Tom knelt and examined the leg.

He pressed down just below the knee. "Does this hurt?"

DeVille screeched.

"It's broken," Tom said. "I'll have to put a splint on it until we can get you to a hospital."

"Do it," DeVille gasped through pained lips.

Tom tore strips of cloth from DeVille's shirt and tied a stiff, light branch to his leg with them. "Best I can do," he said. "Once we get you into town, they'll put a cast on it. You'll be knocking people silly again in no time."

"Thanks, kid," DeVille said with real gratitude. With that, he passed out.

Tom huddled next to Rick on the other side of the pit. "How'd he break his leg?" Rick asked.

"He didn't," whispered Tom. "It's a bad sprain, that's all. But given the pain he's in, he can't tell the difference. He'll be fine in a couple of days, but I don't want him attacking us again tonight, do you?"

Rick shook his head. It was better for them that DeVille think himself helpless.

Tom rested back with his head against a log and closed his eyes. He turned his thoughts to the problems with the disks and the strange ways they might be affecting Rick. That kept him from worrying about what would happen if DeVille awoke in the night, angry and bent on revenge.

Tom's eyes snapped open as he heard a familiar whirring sound. A helicopter hovered overhead, then started to descend, its rotor kicking up an incredible noise. Somehow it knew they were there.

Rick and DeVille were also awake now, shouting at the copter, their voices lost in the noise. But the helicopter was stuck just above the treetops, hindered in its descent. It couldn't get to them. Instead a rope ladder dropped down, dangling in the sky.

Rick leaned close to Tom. "Who is it?"

"Does it matter? They're getting us out of here," Tom said. "You help DeVille up the ladder. I'll be along in a minute."

As Rick and DeVille struggled upward together, Tom scooped up dirt with his hands and dumped it into the pit. Tom stomped out the rest with his shoes, leaving nothing to flare up later. Then he climbed up the rope ladder.

At the top a woman's smooth hand grabbed his and pulled him in. Linda Nueve slid the helicopter door closed and said, "Give me an interview or I shut down your dad's business."

"No way you could do that," Tom said flatly.

"Oh, I don't know," Nueve said confidently. "You watch the place all day, see who's going in and out, put names to faces, it's not too hard to figure out what's going on there. Your dad has a lot of top-secret contracts. I bet if stories about what he's working on leaked out, those contracts would dry up and blow away. Am I right?"

Tom studied her. Nothing on her face suggested she was bluffing.

She laughed. "You've got till we get back to make up your mind. An interview or your dad's career. I'll take one of them with me when I go. It's your choice, Swift."

"How did you find us?" Tom asked, changing the subject. Normally, he wouldn't have been pleased to see her, but at that moment any way out of the forest was okay with him.

Linda Nueve studied him. "You'd make a good reporter, Swift. You ask all the right questions."

"And you stay away from all the answers." Tom pointed at DeVille. "He has to get to a hospital."

"Did these bad boys beat you all up, Danny?" Linda cooed.

DeVille muttered something nasty at her, but Tom barely paid attention. He was more interested in the way she had addressed the kickboxer.

"What's your interest in DeVille?" he asked.

"No interest," DeVille mumbled through teeth clenched together in pain. "She's got no interest at all, except that I'm in the same business as Duke Wellington."

Linda flashed a murderous glance at him, and DeVille snapped his mouth shut.

Tom smiled at Linda with new understanding. "So you and the Duke know each other? Is that how you got onto this story so quickly?"

"I don't know what you're talking about," Linda said bitterly. "There's nothing between Wellington and me. He's a loudmouthed lout and a shabby dresser with bad taste in managers. Anyway, you're mistaken if you think kickboxing isn't big. Maybe it still doesn't outsell football in the sports sections, but it's hot and getting hotter. Look, are you two going to give me an interview or not?"

Tom and Rick exchanged glances, silently comparing thoughts, and Tom shook his head. "No interviews. If you try to publicize the secret contracts my dad is working on, the government will be all over you. And the only reason Rick and I are a story is that you stuck your nose in and made us a story. I didn't want any publicity, and I still don't."

"Ha! Where have you been? Don't you know what's going on in Central Hills?"

Tom looked out the helicopter window. Central Hills Hospital was below now, and as they lowered to the hospital's rooftop helipad, figures in white coats scurried into place on the roof.

"I don't know what you mean," said Tom.

"I don't believe this!" exclaimed Linda Nueve. "You turn a whole sport on its ear, and you don't know what I mean. Everyone who's anyone in kickboxing is pulling into town—Lenny the Phantom, Striker Hayes, Tommy Chi, Roger Salick, just to name a few."

"Wow!" Rick said. Tom and Linda turned to look at him. Tom had never seen such a look of awe on his friend's face. "Those guys are legends. What are they doing here?"

"You really *don't* know," said Linda. "They're here to see your rematch against the champ."

"My *what?*" said Rick.

"Like it or not," Linda Nueve continued, smiling at his reaction, "Central Hills is the new kickboxing capital of the world, and you two put it on the map. Still want to tell me I've got no story?"

Then the helicopter was on the rooftop helipad, its blades slowing to a stop as doctors ducked under them, pulling open the doors. In seconds DeVille was whisked away on a gurney. Other doctors took Tom and Rick aside as Linda Nueve kept a close eye on them.

"Better have your family physician check this out," a doctor told Tom as he examined the bruise where DeVille had struck the pressure point in his shoulder. "There shouldn't be any nerve damage, but it's best to make sure."

"So do I get the interview, or do we set up camp outside your compound again?" Linda Nueve called out, rushing to them as Tom and Rick regrouped at the elevator.

"This isn't a Swift Enterprises project,"

Tom said. The elevator door slid open, and the three of them got on. "Leave my dad's company out of it."

"Yeah?" Linda replied. "The rumor is that you're starting a whole new commercial athletic equipment wing of the company."

"That's not true," Tom blurted. He stopped himself as she grinned, and he realized she was prying information out of him. He composed himself. "It's all my idea, and it won't be marketed."

"Then you'll be the only one with this amazing new training technique? If, in fact, that's what it is?"

"What do you mean, *if* that's what it is?" Rick said angrily. "Of course that's—"

Tom raised a hand, signaling him to stop. "No comment," Tom replied.

The door opened, and they emerged into the ground-floor lobby. "If that's the way you're going to be about it," Linda Nueve said, "I guess we'll be seeing you tomorrow morning. When you look outside your front door, we'll be there."

Tom mulled that over. "So what you're telling me is that you're not going to leave us alone until you've got your interview."

Linda smiled. "That's what I'm telling you, yes."

"And there's no way you can be convinced to forget it?"

"I didn't get where I am today by taking no for an answer," Linda responded. "So when do we do the interview?"

Tom gave in. "Tomorrow morning. At Master Choso's."

Linda looked at Rick. "You'll be there, too?"

Rick nodded sullenly.

"Fine. We'll see you both tomorrow morning." With that she turned on her heel and left.

"If she wants a story so badly," Rick said as he watched her leave, "let's give her a story she'll never forget."

Tom didn't like the sound of that. "What do you mean?"

"Everyone wants me to have a rematch with Wellington," Rick explained. "I'll look chicken if I don't."

"Are you out of your mind?" Tom practically screamed. It wasn't at all like Rick to worry about what people would think, and certainly no one in Central Hills would call Rick a coward for walking away from such a fight. Tom noted this as another incident where Rick's reactions had become erratic and unpredictable and wondered what he could do about it.

"I'm dead serious," Rick said, growing excited as he spoke. "I've been in the ring with the guy, Tom. I know how he fights now. We'll use the cybersuit and tapes, and we'll train as hard and as quickly as we can. With your help I can beat him. What do you say?"

"It's crazy," said Tom. "You said it yourself. He'll *kill* you."

"That was yesterday," Rick said confidently. *Too* confidently, in Tom's opinion. "Today I'm ready for him."

"I can't believe you're actually considering this," Tom said, trying to think of a way to talk Rick out of it. But he saw by the look in Rick's eyes that nothing would be more difficult. With everything he had invented, Tom had yet to invent a way to change Rick Cantwell's mind.

"It's what I want," Rick answered. "I can do it with or without your help, but I'm doing it!"

# 8

CROWDED AROUND A TV MONITOR, THE GROUP leaned forward to watch Wellington's hand snap back and strike with bone-crunching force. His opponent fell back, stunned, and crawled on the mat, trying to find the ropes through his daze. Before Wellington could turn to look at his victim, another man was on him and then a third. Wellington spun and kicked the legs out from under one of them, then ducked under the last man's punch and drove an elbow into the small of his back.

Linda Nueve switched off the videotape. "That's what you're up against," she said. "How do you get ready for something like that?"

They were gathered around a table in the dojo, Linda Nueve and her cameraman on one side, Tom and Rick on the other. Rick seemed calm now, and Tom hoped to keep him that way. They hadn't spoken since the night before, at the hospital. Tom had hoped to talk to Rick before the interview, but the newscaster had arrived too soon.

Master Choso sat on the floor, legs crossed, in a distant corner of the room and silently, intently, watched the proceedings. He had freely given the premises for the interview and disappeared, only to reappear a short time later and take his place in the corner.

Again Tom wondered what he was up to.

"Now," said Linda as the camera began to roll, "tell me about your new training system."

Before Tom could open his mouth, the front door flew open. Through it huffed Johnny Weisel, followed by Duke Wellington and a horde of reporters. "Hold everything," Weisel ordered. "You want to talk to someone, Nueve, you talk to us!"

Linda Nueve stood and turned. Tom didn't think he had ever seen anyone that angry before. "Weisel," she began, "you toad! How did you—"

She stopped as if someone had struck her.

Tom looked up to see her staring numbly into the eyes of Duke Wellington. He stared back, also at a loss for words. To Tom's surprise, Master Choso, forgotten in his corner, was paying close attention to the scene.

"Andy," she said flatly, after what seemed like an eternity.

Impatiently dragging Wellington after him, Weisel stomped around the table. "Ladies and gentlemen of the press"—he glared harshly at Linda—"or whatever you call yourselves, you can forget about these punk kids over here." He half gestured in the direction of Tom and Rick. Then, with a huge grin, he said, "Have we got an announcement for you."

He stepped aside, whispering to Duke Wellington. Then the Duke leaned far over the table, looking out at the reporters. His face tightened into a mask of contempt.

"There are those of you who say I've lost it," the champion bellowed. "There are those who say I'm fair game for any creep who comes along. You think I've been hiding out and not taking on any tough challengers."

"What about Dangerous Danny DeVille?" Linda Nueve called out, to be shushed by other reporters intent on Wellington's every word.

Wellington glared at her. Sensing the moment slipping away, Weisel hurled himself forward. His face reddened as he shouted, "When the Duke says 'creeps,' we all know who he's talking about." He nodded at Rick, and members of the audience murmured knowingly.

"We want this punk to put his teeth where his mouth is," Weisel continued. "Oh, sure, he thinks he can beat the champ. Some people are already trying to pass him off as the new era of kickboxing. But the champ's going to put an end to that once and for all!"

"You said it, Johnny," Wellington said, cutting Weisel off. "Okay, the kid got lucky, I'll give him that. But luck doesn't mean a thing when the mightiest arms in the world are waiting to wrap themselves around your throat." Wellington flexed one arm and displayed a huge knot of a muscle.

"We've got a contract here, punk." Weisel waved some papers at Rick. "Put your John Hancock on it, and we'll put up the belt— or doesn't your mommy let you come out to play?"

"Wait a minute!" shouted a cold voice from behind the reporters. The group parted, making way for Dangerous Danny DeVille to approach the table. He limped slightly, favoring one leg. "If anyone deserves a shot at the champ, it's me!"

The Duke knocked the table aside in a frenzy, almost hitting Tom and Rick with it. "DeVille!" he yelled. "You've been on my case since the day we met! How long are you going to keep sticking your nose in where it isn't wanted?"

"Until your belt is around my waist!" DeVille shouted back. "That's where it belongs, and I'll do anything to put it there."

Tom watched in disbelief as the two monster men of pro kickboxing hurled themselves together, slamming into each other's chests and trying to push the other back, their chins almost touching as they glared murderously into each other's eyes.

"I'll sign," Rick said abruptly. Amid the action he was almost ignored. Then Wellington snapped his head around in a double take.

In that moment of distraction DeVille shoved the Duke back a step.

Johnny Weisel's jaw dropped, but he caught himself before he was noticed and turned his attention to DeVille. "Get out of here, DeVille!" he screamed. "You hack, you washed-up never-was! You get a contract when you've earned one, and not a moment sooner."

DeVille trembled with rage. "And who says when I've earned it?"

"Me," Weisel snapped back. "So get out of here."

"Sure," DeVille said. He hobbled away, little snickers bubbling out of him. As he reached the door, he exploded into laughter. "You'll find out real soon what I've earned, Weisel. Real soon. So you and the fraud go ahead and beat up on kids. I don't care who wins this fight, because whoever the winner is, I'm going to pound him into the mat!"

"Good riddance!" said Johnny Weisel after DeVille had gone. "If there's one thing I hate, it's a creep with a big mouth."

"You said it, Johnny," Wellington agreed. "And speaking of creeps with big mouths, didn't I hear a mouse squeak?"

"You sure did," said Weisel. He slid the contract and a pen to Rick. "Ricky here's going to put his mousy little life on the line."

Rick took the pen, and Tom whispered to him, "You don't have to do this."

Rick looked out at the sea of reporters anxiously waiting for him to sign. "Yes, I do," he whispered back. "I'm no quitter."

"Wait!" Tom said to Weisel. "Let's get one thing straight. This is strictly a grudge match. Nobody makes any money off it."

Weisel's jaw dropped. "But the tickets—even at this short notice—"

"The proceeds from ticket sales go to charity," Tom insisted, "or there's no fight."

"It's okay with me," said Rick.

"Take the deal and let's get on with it, Johnny," ordered the Duke. "The time for talk is over, and the time for pounding has begun," he threatened. Weisel groaned as if he had been hit, but Wellington was paying no attention. He was busy staring down Rick.

"Sign if you've got the guts," Wellington said.

Rick signed.

Immediately Wellington began to laugh, and even Weisel's spirits, deflated in the face of lost income, picked up. "Three days, gentlemen," Weisel announced. "We'll see you there."

Weisel and Wellington marched out. Rapidly the reporters filed out after them.

"Hey!" called Tom as Linda Nueve started through the door. "What about the interview?"

Linda smiled back sweetly. "You were right, Swift. Your system isn't much of a story. If your boy there beats the champ for the title, *then* it's a story."

Then she was gone, leaving Tom and Rick

alone in the room. Rick sat staring at the floor as if in shock.

"Three days," he muttered. "I didn't know it would be so soon. I'll never be able to train in time."

Tom nodded sullenly. "I guess we'd better get started." With a shared sigh they started for the door and the intensive training regimen ahead of them.

"Wait!" cried a voice behind them. It was Master Choso, coming out of the back room. The man usually showed no emotion at all, but now he appeared terrified.

"What is it, Master Choso?" Tom asked. "What's wrong?"

Master Choso was almost trembling as he said, "A phone call. It was Daniel DeVille. He has kidnapped my daughter."

"Tina?"

"He says—" Master Choso stopped, trying to swallow the emotion welling up inside him. "He says that if you do not give him the means to destroy Duke Wellington, I will never see my daughter again."

**R**OBIN MONTAGUE STOOD AT THE BACK DOOR of the kitchen in the Choso apartment, above the dojo. The police chief of Central Hills, she had met the Swift family soon after their arrival and had remained friendly ever since.

"For a guy who teaches self-defense," Robin said, running her fingers up and down the wooden door frame, "you sure don't have very good security." Wood splayed out in the screwholes where a chain had been torn from the frame. "And you, Tom—you should have filed a report on that helicopter hijacking. Between the two of you, you're almost as much to blame for Tina's kidnapping as De-Ville is."

Master Choso bristled at the accusation, and Tom stepped in to stop an argument.

"I figured I'd put DeVille out of commission, at least for a while," Tom apologized. "What could we have gotten him on? Destruction of private property? I wrecked the helicopter as much as he did. On something like that, he'd be out on bail by now, anyway."

"How about kidnapping?" said Robin. "He snatched you and Rick without your permission. That's a major offense. So is hijacking an aircraft. We could have locked him up for a while."

She faced Master Choso. "And we will, once we've caught him. Odds are he'll call you again, to set up a meeting, so I want to put a tap on your phone. Is that all right? When someone calls, it will automatically tell us the number that the call is coming from."

Master Choso nodded sullenly. "Yes."

Robin turned back to Tom. "And I don't want you even thinking about giving in to this DeVille. No swaps. A lot of times people give in to kidnappers and still never see the victims again." Then, seeing Master Choso's sinking face: "Don't get me wrong, Mr. Choso. I don't have any reason to believe we won't get your daughter back, safe and sound."

She started out the door, then looked back

in. "Mr. Choso, don't make any promises when he calls back. Tom, keep yourself available. If it's your property he's after, DeVille may want you to do the swap."

Tom listened to her footsteps going down the stairs. Master Choso sank into a chair, desolate.

"I'm sorry," Tom said. "This is my fault."

"No," said Master Choso after some thought. "The blame is mine. I played a game and lost control of it."

"What do you mean?" asked Tom, genuinely puzzled.

"When we first arrived in Central Hills, you approached me with your friend, Rick," Master Choso explained. "Rick wanted to learn the art of kickboxing. You, however, sought only the knowledge, not the art, and you sought it hungrily, without patience."

"Well, there's a lot to know," Tom cut in. "These are my prime learning years."

"No," Master Choso corrected. "A man never stops learning. In this community I am regarded as a master of the martial arts. But there are those to whom my knowledge is but the knowledge of a child. I, too, hope to share their knowledge, their skill, one day. I may live to be a hundred without mastering half of what they have mastered."

Tom began to speak, but Master Choso raised his palm, signaling Tom to silence. He continued. "I am of the old ways. In my world the unaided human body is the perfect tool, the perfect weapon. Great emphasis is placed on natural achievement, the perfection of the *spirit* rather than the perfect body armor.

"But you, when you first came to see me, were obviously in love with your technology. In your eyes I saw not a love for the form, the art of kickboxing. I could see you wanted the training not for its own sake but for how you could apply it to your other ideas. You did not want to learn the art, you wanted to reinvent it."

"Which, I guess, is what I've done. Was that wrong?" Tom asked.

"Some might take it as an insult, though I am sure it was not intended that way. You must have felt my hostility—"

"I did," said Tom. "Frankly, it didn't make any sense to me."

"—and so you stayed away. I knew what you would do. You had no malice in your heart, and you wished to win me over the only way you knew how, through your technology. When you came to me with your device, the training invention, I was appalled."

"You sure didn't show it," Tom said.

"No." For the first time since Tina was kidnapped, Master Choso smiled, just a little bit. "The best preparation for attack is to keep your opponents unaware of what you are going to do."

"I didn't know we were opponents."

"We didn't need to be," Master Choso said sadly. "That was entirely my fault. But you must understand—from my point of view, training in the art *must* be accomplished slowly, step by step. It is a long, elaborate, and often tedious process."

"But that's what I was trying to eliminate!" said Tom. "Think how many more people would swamp to kickboxing if it wasn't so difficult."

"The difficulty is the *essence* of the art," Master Choso explained. He had lapsed back into his calm teaching voice, a sign to Tom that he was getting past the initial stress of the situation. "I seek to master it, you seek to go around it. Do you not understand the difference in our approaches?"

"So you're saying I was wrong," Tom stated flatly.

"I am saying . . ." Master Choso paused a moment, carefully selecting his words. "You chose a path that I would not. Another who chose a path I would not was Duke Wellington. Your invention and your eagerness to test it coincided with my former student's visit. I thought to teach two lessons at once."

"Lessons in what?" Tom asked. He didn't know whether to be angry or fascinated.

Master Choso's head sank. "Humility. Perhaps it is I who needed the lesson in humility." Then, far softer: "Perhaps this is my lesson."

"We're not beaten yet," Tom said. "I have a plan. I don't know if it will work or not. We need videotapes of Dangerous Danny De-Ville—fighting, sparring, whatever. Do you have any friends in the kickboxing world who might have tapes?"

Master Choso crooked a finger and motioned Tom to follow him. They passed down a short, dark hallway into the living room of the apartment. An antique Oriental rug covered the floor, and at the far end of the room was a tall wooden cabinet.

Master Choso pulled down the blinds, cutting out most of the light into the room. He hit a wall switch, and to Tom's surprise, a screen descended from the ceiling near him. Master Choso opened the wooden cabinet. On the bottom shelf, with a videocassette recorder sitting on top of it, was a video projector, aimed at the screen. The upper shelves were filled with dozens of videotapes.

"Master Choso, you old dog." Tom laughed. "A projection television system, after all that talk about how much you hated technology."

"I like television," Master Choso said simply.

He rooted among the shelves and in moments came out with several tapes. He held one up. "This features DeVille against Andrew Wellington in the finals of the North American competition two years ago."

"Wellington won?"

"Yes. Andrew has always beaten Mr. DeVille." Master Choso held up a second tape. "In this, DeVille fought in a special challenge series in Hong Kong. Andrew did not participate for personal reasons."

"DeVille won that one?" Tom asked.

"No," replied Master Choso, and a wave of sadness and regret swept over him again. "He was disqualified for cheating and for unnecessary brutality." Covering his eyes with a hand, he handed the remaining tapes to Tom.

"I wouldn't worry about it too much," Tom said. "DeVille is certainly serious about winning at kickboxing, and he may talk a good game, but I don't think he's a killer. I doubt he'll hurt one hair on— Whoa!"

Tom looked at a beat-up videotape box. The words on it were in Chinese, and he didn't know what they said, but also on it was a picture of a small girl in a classic martial arts pose. "This is Tina!" Tom said.

Master Choso snatched the box away. Then his arms sagged by his side. "This is a day for telling secrets," he said.

Tom took the box back. "I didn't know she kickboxed."

"She doesn't want it known," Master Choso said. "She began training almost as soon as she was old enough to walk. When I became a champion, she came into the spotlight, too, and soon she was well-known as one of the best junior kickboxers, an unusual feat for a girl. But the other children no longer knew how to deal with her, and she . . ."

He fell silent. "She grew so lonely. This is one of the reasons we moved here, to Central Hills. She made me promise to tell no one of her past, so that other teenagers would think of her as one of them and not someone special."

Tom fingered the box, thinking things over. "I'd like to take this tape of Tina with me," he said. "Don't worry. I won't let anyone else see it, and there's no reason for Tina to know you told me anything about her." He picked up the other tapes as well.

Master Choso studied him gratefully. "Thank you. But what can you do that the police cannot?"

"Plenty, if I'm right," Tom said. "I'll let you know. Stay here around the phone, and give me a call if you hear from DeVille. I'm available if you need me."

He started for the door, then stopped abruptly. "Something I'm curious about," Tom said to Master Choso. "How did you get Wellington into this, anyway? It seems to me a man like Wellington has better things to do than spar with teenagers."

Master Choso smiled slyly. "Andrew owes me a great debt. I thought this a good opportunity to collect on it."

"What kind of debt?" Tom pressed. "Sure, you were his teacher, but—"

"This is between you and me," Master Choso said. It was an order, not a request. "My daughter was of great concern to me. I wanted her to have a home, with friends of her own age. This was not possible while I was kickboxing champion. We were on the road all the time, traveling from match to match. I wished to retire. But as long as I remained undefeated I was required to defend the title. To have simply retired without allowing the next challenger his chance to *win* the title would have been an insult to both of us."

Tom tried to make sense of the master's words. What did all that have to do with Wellington? Then it hit him. Rick had said Wellington had won the championship from Master Choso! "You threw the fight?" Tom blurted in disbelief. "The Duke is the champ because you allowed him to win?"

"My daughter is important to me," Master Choso said, avoiding the question. "Please do what you can to help her."

Tom knew he would get nothing else on the subject out of Master Choso.

Leaving him by the phone in his living room, Tom took the videotapes and hurried out of the apartment and down the back stairs. Sprinting down the alley, Tom hoped it wouldn't take long to find Tina. With the match three nights off, most of Tom's time would be eaten up just getting Rick ready for the fight.

He had, in fact, already sent Rick off to the Swift gymnasium, where Sandra was waiting for him. Tom had explained the workings of his training system to her that morning before he left for the interview, and while she thought it was all a waste of time, she was more than willing to spend her days with Rick, especially if it was a way to help him out.

Tom walked out to the black van that he used as a mobile lab. As he stuck the key in the door, Tom was suddenly aware of a trap, but it was too late. Huge, steely fingers clamped around the back of his neck. Tom winced in pain, and the pain turned to darkness. Just before he passed out, Tom thought he could hear Duke Wellington saying, "I said I'd find you later. Welcome to later, kid."

**T**OM AWOKE.

He was amazed to find himself behind the wheel of his own van. Even more amazing was the round little man seated next to him and the angry face glowering at him in his rearview mirror.

"I don't have time for this," he said, rubbing his neck where Wellington had squeezed it. "Dangerous Danny DeVille—"

"Forget DeVille," Johnny Weisel said. "We have. If you know what's good for you, we'll take a little trip together and you'll do as you're told."

Wellington leaned forward, his hot breath on the back of Tom's neck. "We're old pals, you and us, see? You're going to take your old pals right into your lab, so we can get a close-up look at that so-called cyborg kickboxer of yours."

"Now, why would I want to do that?" Tom asked.

"Because I'm in the mood to break something," Wellington said. "It's either you or your machine. Take your pick."

Casually Tom pulled out into the street. As he drove, he glanced in his rearview mirror and noticed a van pull out into the street a block behind him.

"You didn't have to assault me," Tom said, as they cruised through Central Hills. "If you wanted me to take you to the lab, you could have just asked."

Weisel snorted. "We don't ask, punk. We tell."

"So what do you think you'll get by smashing my equipment? I can always build more."

"But maybe not in time for the match," Weisel said with smug confidence.

"Maybe we should smash you, too, kid," said Wellington. "Is that what you're trying to tell us?"

"Rick used to say such great things about you, Duke," Tom said with a touch of distaste. "You were a real hero of his. Look at you. All you are now is just another bully."

"That's *Mr.* Duke to you, creep," Wellington said. "Rick? That's whatsisname, right?"

"Yeah. Rick Cantwell. He's the guy who decked you," Tom said. He couldn't keep a smile hidden when Wellington's embarrassment was reflected in the mirror.

The van turned a corner and started up a gentle incline toward the foothills where Swift Enterprises nestled.

"Your pal's got great taste in heroes," Weisel said. "And lousy taste in friends."

"I would have thought it was the other way around," Tom said. "By the way, do either of you know why someone's following us?"

Wellington wrapped an arm around Tom's neck and squeezed slightly. "If you're conning us, kid, I'll snap your neck like a toothpick."

"Look for yourself," Tom said.

Weisel popped his head out the window. "It's no con," he said. "Looks like another van, all right."

Duke Wellington stiffened. "What kind of van?"

Tom pretended to crane for a better look, although he had recognized the van.

"Looks like there are TV call letters on top," said Tom. "Yeah, that's it. Some kind of news crew, I'd say."

"Linda," croaked Wellington. "What's *she* doing here?"

"Ask the boy genius," Weisel replied.

"Don't look at me," Tom said. "I didn't want any publicity. I didn't even want *you* involved. That was Master Choso's idea."

"Shut up and drive," Weisel ordered, scowling out his window. "How long do we have to ride through this hick burg? Can't you speed it up a little?"

Tom grinned and turned a corner. They had reached the spot he'd been waiting for, a barren access road leading to the gates of the Swift complex. Tom hit a button underneath the steering column and said, "I'll see what I can do."

For a split second the van jerked to a halt as the systems switched over to turbo. Weisel opened his mouth in outrage, but before he could speak, the van took off like a shot, and the little manager's expression twisted to horror.

Tom clung to the steering wheel as the van roared down the access road. Telephone poles and street lamps turned into blurred smudges of light and shadow as they whipped past.

"Stop it!" the Duke shouted. He straightened up and reached again for Tom's neck, but Tom saw the hands coming.

"I wouldn't do that," Tom said. "We're going 227 miles per hour and climbing. If anything happens to me at this speed, you end up an inkblot on the sidewalk."

Wellington pulled back his hands and slouched into the seat in silent terror. Neither he nor Weisel had any way of knowing that the van was locked into a computer guidance system that would steer it far better than Tom ever could. On this road with no cross streets, driveways, or unauthorized traffic, there was no way the van could crash—unless Tom wanted it to.

Then Swift Enterprises came into view. Both Wellington and Weisel relaxed, confident that Tom would slow down. He didn't. The van raced ever closer to the gate.

Closer.

Closer.

They were on top of it. Security guards, seeing the van coming, hurled themselves out of the way. Weisel screamed. Tom hit the switch on a small black box on his visor.

The gate rose up. The van zipped through it, heading for the wall of a building. Weisel wouldn't stop screaming, and now Wellington joined him.

Weisel grabbed for the steering wheel.

Tom knocked Weisel's arm aside and

slammed on the brakes. They locked, and unknown to the Duke or his manager, computer guidance clicked into place. The van went into a spin, careening at the waiting concrete wall. With a whoosh, jets of air shot out through pneumatic pumps along the van's underbelly, bringing the van to a screeching halt with air pressure.

It was over in seconds. The digital readout on Tom's speedometer plunged from over 250 miles per hour to zero. But the van still rolled, carried forward by its own momentum. One last thing was needed to bring the van to a complete halt, and it was the thing Tom Swift was counting on.

Very gently the bumper tapped the wall. The van stopped.

Tom had timed it perfectly. He dived out his door as air bags, triggered by the collision, mushroomed through the van's interior, pinning Weisel and Wellington in their seats.

Now that it was over, Tom found his hands shaking. It had been close, too close. If his calculations had been off by even a fraction . . .

He heard voices now and saw a number of people running for him. Among them were his sister and Rick.

"Boy, are you going to be in trouble when

Dad hears about this!" Sandra said, eyes on the van.

"I think he'll understand," said Tom. "Could you go to the gate and tell them a news van should arrive there any minute? Tell them to let the woman in and escort her to the lab, okay?"

"I don't see why I have to do it."

"Please," Tom said.

She grinned. "Well, as long as you ask so nicely. Come on, Rick."

"No," Tom said. "I need Rick here. After you're done up front, round up Dan Coster. We're going to need him."

As Sandra went to the gate, Tom said to the van, "Deflate." As the air bags hissed and collapsed back into their holders, Tom swallowed a chuckle. Rick was batting his eyes in disbelief as Wellington and Weisel appeared from under the shrinking bags.

"You should never get in a stranger's van," Tom scolded jokingly.

"I'll sue!" blustered Johnny Weisel, trying desperately to straighten his mussed hair. "Your old man's going to pay through the nose."

"Shut up," Wellington told his manager. Facing the behemoth, the little man swallowed hard and shrank back. Wellington turned to Tom. "That little stunt sure took guts, kid. I don't respect much, but guts I respect." For the first time Wellington stretched out an open hand to Rick. "I guess that goes for you, too."

"I don't believe this!" Weisel shrieked. "This nice guy stuff won't keep the heavy-weight belt around your waist! These guys are the enemy, you got that? The enemy!"

The Duke ignored him. "Sorry for all the trouble, kid," he told Tom. "I guess we'll be going now. No hard feelings, okay?"

"None at all," Tom said. "But aren't you forgetting something?"

"What's that?"

"You came here to destroy my invention," answered Tom. "Hadn't you better do that?"

Rick, Weisel, and the Duke just stared at him. Then, with a grin, Tom led them in the direction of his lab.

To Tom it was clear that neither Weisel nor Wellington understood a word he was saying. He held a disk in one hand, explaining the way the system worked. His lecture was met with blank stares.

"You've heard of an exoskeleton?" he said finally.

Johnny Weisel's eyes lit up. "Sure! One of those mechanical suits you wear that make you stronger." He gave a big smile, obviously pleased with his own knowledge.

"That's one way to put it," said Tom, who had never heard it put that way before. "Think of a lot of these disks and the fiber-optic mesh they rest in as a suit, but instead of using mechanical strength amplification, the disks form a cybernetic link with the nervous system that amplifies skill."

"You lost me," Wellington said.

"He's been losing me since the day I met him," said Rick. "You get used to it."

The intercom buzzed, and Tom went to open the door to the lab. A uniformed guard led Linda Nueve into the room by the arm. "Let go of me," she demanded, but she froze when she saw who was in the room. The guard left the room, shutting the door behind him.

"Linda," Duke Wellington said.

She nodded. "Andy."

Tom and Rick glanced at each other.

"How have you been?" asked Wellington.

"I'm fine," she replied, and then she seemed to sag with exhaustion. "Listen to us. We sound like a couple of strangers."

"It's been a long time," Wellington replied.

Linda eyed Weisel with annoyance. "I see he's still mooching off you."

"You never understood," said the Duke.

"A fighter's got to have a manager, that's the way it is. Because of him I won the championship."

"No. Because of *you* you won the championship. You could have done it with any manager. You didn't need this little jerk."

"Hey!" Weisel protested. "You're just mad because he didn't pick you."

"You're right I'm mad," Linda said. "If I had managed him, he'd be a champion people were proud of. And I wouldn't have treated him like my personal feed bag."

"I don't have to take this," Johnny Weisel protested. He wagged a finger at Wellington. "If you want to give an interview to an old sportscaster pal, Duke, it's fine with me. But don't you dare think about switching management!"

"I wasn't thinking about it," Wellington replied. "Until now."

Weisel fumed. "We've got a contract, and you're keeping it. If you want to stay in the sport, you'll wreck the kid's experiment right now because there are plenty of guys out there who want to take you down. If the creep wins again, every one of them will be out to get their hands on that ... that ... whatever it is!"

He stormed off, and Tom hit the intercom

button on the telephone on the wall. "Harlan," he said to the security chief on the other end, "someone's coming out. See that he gets shown out of the complex. Thanks."

Tom held up a disk. "Sorry to change the subject, but we have more pressing matters at hand. You were going to wreck these, remember?"

Wellington shook his head. "That was Johnny's idea."

Tom shrugged and set the disk back down. "Suit yourself. I was going to dismantle the system, anyway."

Rick's jaw dropped. "Why?"

"Because I need the parts," Tom explained. "Dangerous Danny DeVille has kidnapped Tina Choso."

"Tina?" interjected Wellington. He was dumbfounded.

"Yes," said Tom. He pried open a disk, held it up to the light, and squinted at it.

"Uh-oh," said Rick. "Tom has that inventing look in his eye again."

"That's right," Tom said. "When I'm done, it'll be the end of Dangerous Danny DeVille once and for all."

He started to work, wondering if anyone heard him say, under his breath, "Or the end of me."

**11**

"MAYBE WE SHOULD LEAVE FINDING TINA TO the police," Linda Nueve said a few hours later. By then Dan Coster had arrived, and Harlan Ames had also volunteered to join the desperate search.

"The police don't have my equipment," Tom said. He was in one corner of the lab, supervising a team of robots. "What I've put together won't lead us right to her, but it should cut the search time drastically. We know all people have identifying marks, like fingerprints or the patterns of their corneas—"

Sandra yawned. "Or their voiceprints and heartbeats. Get to the point."

Tom was impressed. "How did you know?"

"I saw what you were doing," Sandra explained. "You were dismantling the visual sensors in your disk system and replacing them with audio sensors. What else could you be going for?"

"I get it," said Rick. "We find Tina by her heartbeat." He looked pleased with himself, then his brow furrowed in thought. "How do we do that?"

"With these." Tom held up one of the black boxes that the robots had been putting together. "They're hypersensitive microphone-transmitters. Of my own design, of course. They'll pick up any sound, even those the human ear can't hear, and they make a digital recording of the sound, reducing the elements of sound to computer codes."

"Which are transmitted back to the Swift Enterprises mainframe, if your training disks are any indication," said Sandra, attempting to speed him along.

"Where the digital codes are sorted out by the computer and checked for a match against the target code." Tom continued as if there had been no interruption. "I've set up a demonstration."

Tom triggered the remote control for his wall TV system, and a videotape began to play. It was a recording of Tom and Rick sparring in Tom's gym. As they fought, sounds were stripped away—first their voices, then the slapping of their bodies on the mat, then the room echoes and all other noises, until nothing was left but the beating of their hearts.

The picture froze and vanished from the screen. After a flash of darkness it was replaced by a computer-simulated map of Central Hills as seen from overhead. The map blinked in closer and closer, focusing first on the neighborhood housing Swift Enterprises, then on the complex itself. It locked there, a red arrow pulsing at the specific location of Tom's lab.

"See, the computer first got a recording of our heartbeats. Then this"—Tom held up the black box again—"picked up our heartbeats now, relayed the data back to the computer, and the computer correlated the data to determine our current locations."

"So that thing can listen to Central Hills and find Tina's location, right?" asked Dan Coster.

"That's what I need you for," Tom answered. "The black boxes have a short range, a couple of hundred yards at best. We're going to have to methodically canvass all of

Central Hills until we come across Tina and DeVille."

"That's why you focused on heartbeat," Sandra said. "If neither of them is talking, we could go right past them and never pick up their voiceprints. But you can't shut off a heartbeat."

Linda Nueve cut in. "This is all very impressive, but how do you know they're still in Central Hills?"

"I don't," replied Tom. "It's an educated guess. DeVille wants something from me, and the farther he goes from Central Hills, the harder it will be to get it. I'm willing to bet he's still here—and we can nab him."

"There's just one thing I don't understand," Dan said. "Where do we get a digital of Tina's heartbeat? Or DeVille's?"

Like a magician pulling a rabbit out of his hat, Tom produced the videotape of DeVille. "I've already put the computer to work stripping out the data we need on DeVille. As for Tina, her father gave us that information. That's all I can tell you. Tina's heartbeat is the primary target, DeVille's the secondary one. They may not be in the same place, so we're programmed for both of them."

"Then we're set," said Rick. "Let's divide up the town and start cruising."

Tom started handing out the boxes. When he passed Wellington and Linda Nueve, the champ said, "Don't I get one?"

Tom looked him over. "Sure your manager will allow it? Shouldn't you be in training?"

"If Johnny doesn't like it, he can stuff it," Wellington growled. "DeVille's been pulling stunts like this for a long time. You track him down," concluded the Duke. "After that, he's mine."

Tom switched the steering of his van to the on-board computer and leaned back to relax. The computer kept it cruising at a steady speed of thirty miles per hour, scanning speed limit signs as it went along to raise or lower the speed of the car. Built-in radar scanned for obstacles; in computer mode the car could stop on a dime.

At Tom's command the digital sound system clicked in with a barrage of hard rock. It was time to think.

The search party had gone off in pairs, for the most part: Rick and Sandra, Wellington and Linda Nueve—plus her ever-present cameraman—and Dan Coster and Harlan Ames, leaving Tom on his own. Driving up and down the streets of Central Hills had left Tom with nothing but a realization of how large his hometown really was.

No one else had any luck, either. If any of the boxes had picked up Tina's heartbeat or DeVille's, a light would have signaled all of them. But there had been no light. Tom was starting to think that DeVille had left town after all.

Think, he told himself. DeVille was a flamboyant character. Tom couldn't see him staying cooped up for long. DeVille wasn't the sort of man who'd run, and Tom felt correct in assuming he was still in Central Hills. He'd stay and fight, insisting he could beat anyone. In a place like Central Hills, where he was a stranger, where would DeVille hide with a teenage girl?

Suddenly a yellow light on Tom's black box began to blink. It wasn't the signal he had been waiting for. Only Tom's box had this light, an indicator that someone was trying to reach him on his home phone.

He switched the van back to manual, pulled over to the curb, and picked up the red cellular phone. It was his hot line back to the Swift complex. At the other end the Swift Enterprises computer intercepted his call and rerouted it to the number that had just called him.

"Chief Montague's office," said a friendly male voice.

"This is Tom Swift," Tom said. "I think the chief was trying to get in touch with me."

There was silence for a second. Then Robin Montague came on, saying, "Tom, where are you? He called."

"DeVille? You spoke with him?"

"I heard the tape," Robin said. "He spoke with Choso, wouldn't let him get a word in edgewise."

"Did you trace where he was calling from?"

"A phone booth across from the west entrance to Florio Park," said Robin. "He was gone by the time we got there."

The park, Tom thought. Would he be hiding out there? It was unlikely, he decided. DeVille would want better cover, maybe somewhere near there.

Tom's mind began racing. "What did he say to Choso?"

"He wanted you to be at Choso's with your disks and the rest of the equipment in an hour, or else. He left that part up to the imagination. When he calls in an hour, he'll tell you where to meet him and when."

"Sounds like he's planning to run me all around town," Tom replied.

"Looks like it. DeVille doesn't want the

police involved, and Choso has decided he doesn't want us involved, either."

"So it's up to me."

"If we play it the way DeVille wants, yes," Robin said. "How do you want to play it?"

"I've got an idea," said Tom. "If you don't hear from me, I'll be at Choso's in an hour."

He hung up the phone. He figured DeVille wouldn't be hiding in the park, but the park bordered on a new development—a shopping and business complex on a massive scale, designed by the Central Hills city government to lure new businesses into the area. The complex was half finished, and the construction area covered four city blocks. Besides offices and stores, the development featured a multiplex of theaters and a convention center. In the convention center they were building an arena.

Tom started up the van and sped off, thinking about what he had just learned from Chief Montague. The construction area was fenced off to traffic, and the convention center was in the core of the development. It was far beyond the range of his black box.

Ten minutes later Tom pulled up outside the construction site. It was tightly locked. He peered through the chicken-wire fence. He could see nothing moving inside, and nothing registered on his black box. He tried the lock on the gate. It was shut tight.

He studied the high fence. No one could scale that carrying a young woman. Tom had to face the fact that he was wrong.

Then he noticed the chicken wire in the fence. In one corner the edges of the chicken wire had been doubled over to make a smooth edge to the pole frame. At a casual glance it looked completely normal. Tentatively Tom pressed his fingers against it.

It pushed aside. Someone had made his own gate next to the front gate, and Tom had a good idea who that someone was. He quickly went back to his van and took a canvas carryall from the back, a carryall that held a spare set of disk meshes and linkup equipment. If he did run into DeVille here, he knew he would need all the bargaining chips he could produce.

Tom stepped through the exposed hole and carefully walked through the construction site. Then he saw it, ahead in the distance: the convention center. Quickly he walked forward, holding the black box in front of him. The convention center was almost within its range.

On his black box the light flashed red.

## 12

**A**NXIOUSLY TOM WAITED. THEN AN LED PANEL came alive, and across it scrolled a digital readout identifying two heartbeats and their location.

Both Tina Choso and Dangerous Danny DeVille were in there.

Tom checked his watch. Half an hour had passed since he had spoken to Chief Montague. DeVille would be leaving soon to call Master Choso's, expecting to find Tom there. Should I go in now, Tom wondered, or should I wait for DeVille to leave?

DeVille made the decision for him. The rock-solid man with the strange haircut emerged from the convention center and headed right for him.

Tom ducked behind a wall and held his breath as DeVille walked by. Tom counted slowly to ten, then exhaled in a fierce burst. When he looked around, DeVille was nowhere to be seen.

Tom hurried into the convention center. It was even less finished than the other buildings, and what walls there were blocked much of the late afternoon sun. There was no sign of Tina.

Then he heard her call out, "Tom! Down here!"

He stopped. At his feet was a ten-foot-deep concrete pit. In the middle of the pit, looking up at him, was Tina.

"DeVille took the ladder and left me stranded," she explained.

"I'll get you out," said Tom. Then something smashed into his back, staggering him. The carryall snapped away from his arm, and he was falling.

Go limp, he told himself as he plunged through empty air. Instinctively he righted himself and landed catlike on his feet in the bottom of the pit.

"Are you all right?" Tina asked, rushing to his side.

Tom nodded. Then he looked up and saw DeVille standing at the rim of the pit.

"Good thing I came back," he mocked. He pulled a disk from Tom's carryall and gleefully stuck it against his forehead like a third eye. "Now I've got the means to crush Duke Wellington."

"And *I've* got *you*," came a brusque voice from behind him.

Tom could hardly believe his ears. DeVille looked as astonished as Tom was.

It was Duke Wellington. At the edge of the pit, he assumed a fighting stance. "You've wanted this for a long time, DeVille. Come on. Let's do it."

DeVille backed away, his hands rummaging through Tom's carryall as he kept his wary eyes on the Duke. "This isn't what I wanted, and you know it, Wellington. When I smash you, I want to do it in front of an audience."

Tom saw Linda Nueve approach the two fighters, her cameraman in tow. "How about a *worldwide* audience?" she asked DeVille.

"So you two got back together, huh?" DeVille said. "You deserve each other. I'm glad you're going to see what a wimp your hubby is."

"Leave her out of this," the Duke warned.

"Excuse me," Tom said from the pit.

"What?" DeVille yelled at Tom. "We're busy here."

Tom put an arm around Tina and drew her near. "Do you think we could get out of this pit now?"

"Not a chance," DeVille told Tom. "I still owe you for that broken-leg bit up in the hills. As soon as I'm done with this washed-up clown, it's payback time for you."

The champ smiled faintly. "Okay, Danny boy. Any way you want it, that's how we'll do it."

DeVille charged. The Duke backed up two steps and waited for DeVille to come into his arms. Squaring off, Wellington delivered a left jab at the same time DeVille threw one. Both missed, but it brought Wellington into a clinch, his chest tight against DeVille's.

Too late DeVille realized what was happening. The Duke had already wrapped his left elbow around DeVille's right wrist and brought his left knee up alongside DeVille's hip. With his right arm over the Dangerous One's shoulder and down his back, Wellington turned away suddenly, pivoting into a hip throw.

DeVille flew up in the air and over onto his back as Wellington spun and kicked out his right leg. A moment later, DeVille was on the floor on his back, his wrist still trapped in Wellington's elbow. Wellington stood in a half squat, legs spaced, and his free fist up to deliver an end blow.

Before the blow could fall, DeVille snaked his body violently and launched himself back to his feet, pulling his wrist free of Wellington's grip.

As the two men struggled, Tom could glimpse Linda's cameraman taping the fight.

DeVille struck with a right roundhouse kick to Wellington's midsection. As Wellington doubled over, DeVille swept his foot up, catching the champ on the side of the head. The champ staggered back, and DeVille swept his legs out from under him and then drove his knuckles at Wellington's neck.

Wellington rolled aside, the blow harmlessly glancing off his shoulder. DeVille came at him again, and Wellington rolled again and again—over the lip of the pit.

"No!" screamed Tina. "Uncle Andy!"

Wellington's fingertips latched on to the edge, and he appeared to freeze in midfall, defying gravity. The Duke swept out his legs as he rolled back up onto the floor. Now it was DeVille who lost his footing as the Duke's legs plowed through him.

Cautiously the two men came to their feet and studied each other. Neither moved.

"Uncle Andy?" Tom said to Tina.

Despite the tension of the moment, she giggled. "He's not really my uncle, of course. But when I was growing up, he trained with my father. We saw each other often," she said. Then she turned sad. "He still visits occasionally, but he's not like he used to be. He seems more concerned about being champion, less interested in the people he used to love. I wish the old Uncle Andy would return."

"Something tells me he's trying to," Tom said. "Maybe we can help him."

Tom could see Wellington and DeVille near the lip of the pit, sizing each other up. Each was completely focused on the other.

"Linda!" Tom shouted. "Help us get out of here."

The newscaster darted to the pit. "Can't it wait? There's a fight going on here."

"Do you have any cable?" asked Tom. "Something strong?"

"What?" She had been watching Wellington. "Oh. No. The camcorder's on a battery pack, and the microphone works by radio transmission."

Tom scowled and took off his shirt and his belt. Worrying the thread with his teeth, he tore the sleeves off the shirt, then ripped the remaining fabric in half down the middle. He quickly knotted the pieces into a long cord and yanked at it, testing it. He crouched and untied his shoes, pulling the laces free. With the laces he tied his belt to the shirt.

To Tina he explained, "With luck this will be long enough, and I think it'll hold." To Linda Tom called, "Catch."

Linda Nueve caught the end as he threw it past her. It dangled partway down the ten-foot-deep pit, ending just out of Tom's reach.

"We'll have to jump for it," Tom said. "Hold on tight, Linda."

"You're nuts!" Linda said. "This thing can't support your weight, and even if it does, I don't think I can."

"Get someone else to help you."

Linda Nueve looked at Duke Wellington, but he was on the move now.

"Duke's busy," Linda said to Tom. "I don't think we could get DeVille to help, and the only other person here is—" She glanced at the cameraman, who was intently videotaping the fight. Then she sighed, put her hands on her hips, and called, "Billy! Drop the camera and get over here!"

She held the makeshift rope, and her cameraman got a grip, too.

Before Tom wrapped his arms around Tina's waist and lifted her up, she put her arms around his neck and gave him a peck on the cheek. "For luck," she said softly.

Tom smiled and said nothing. Then Tina had the cord and was pulling herself from the pit.

By the time Tom made it to the top, DeVille and Wellington were locked in combat again. DeVille threw a right punch. Wellington stepped inside the blow and knocked it aside. Again he grabbed DeVille's arm as it went by, and using DeVille's momentum against him, the Duke spun and flung DeVille to the ground.

"It's a lot different when you're not wearing gloves," Wellington taunted. "Isn't it, *Daniel?*"

DeVille started to get angry, but choked his anger back. "Don't worry about me, *Andrew*. I'm just warming up."

"Is that what you call it?" said Wellington. He launched into a series of kicks that drove DeVille back.

Up against a wall DeVille stumbled and dropped to his hands and knees. From where he watched, Tom could see the terror in DeVille's eyes, as if DeVille knew he was doing his best against Wellington and had learned that his best would never be enough.

Then a crafty smile crossed DeVille's lips.

He ducked low as the Duke's foot sliced the air over his head. DeVille rolled forward through Wellington's legs, one arm reaching into shadows.

Sensing DeVille's desperation, Duke Wellington twirled and with a bloodchilling scream launched himself into a flying kick. He sailed through the air like a human arrow.

Just as Wellington reached him, DeVille sidestepped and swung both his arms around like a baseball batter swinging at the ball. In his hands was a two-by-four—lumber from the construction. It splintered as it smacked into the champ's back. Wellington fell to the floor in a groaning heap.

"Duke!" cried Linda Nueve. She began to run to him.

Tina grabbed her shoulder and yanked her back. "Stay here with Tom. I'll help Uncle Andy."

Laughing, DeVille hit Wellington with the board once again. With the Duke helpless at his feet, he dropped the board and scooped up Tom's carryall. From it he drew the disk-meshed shirt. Quickly, he stripped to the waist and pulled it on.

"The kid was wearing this when he knocked your head in," DeVille told Wellington. "Think what'll be left of you when someone who knows what he's doing wears it." He grabbed Wellington's hair and pulled his head up so they were eye to eye. "Let's find out, why don't we?"

"You don't earn the right to fight him until you get by me!" Tina yelled. Startled, DeVille spun toward her. When he saw her, he laughed.

"Go away, cutie," he said. "If Wellington can't stand up to me, what chance do you think you have?"

In answer she was on him, delivering a hard kick to his chest. He staggered back, stunned, his eyes bugging out. To Tom he looked as if he would explode with rage.

DeVille rushed at Tina, kicking and punching. With grace that Tom had never witnessed before, Tina sidestepped DeVille's every move. She dropped and caught the floor with her hands. Her legs swung out. DeVille leapt over them, drawing his knees tight to his chest. Tina sprang up behind him as he landed. Jerking her arm forward and shotgunning it back with a twist, she drove her elbow into the small of his back.

DeVille screamed. Tina spun, catching him on the back of the neck with one high kick after another. DeVille stuck out a fist and twirled as hard as he could. Tina ducked, planted a tiger's claw knucklepunch in De-Ville's ribs, and cartwheeled out of reach.

DeVille gasped for air and gaped at her. "You're just a kid," he muttered as his rage mounted.

"Yes," said Tina as she darted in and snapped DeVille's head back with a wheel kick. "And if I hadn't been knocked unconscious by the door when you kicked it in, this *kid* would have put you in traction!"

"Don't feel too bad, Daniel," said Wellington, who was now on his feet. "I don't know that I could beat her myself. You forget she's Master Choso's daughter."

"Choso?" DeVille shrieked in outrage. "Choso's an old fraud—wouldn't teach me—couldn't teach anybody." He stood half doubled over, sucking in air and holding his ribs, as Tina slowly approached him from one side and Wellington from the other. His fingers struck a disk on his side, and anger flooded through him again as he turned to Tom.

"It doesn't work!" he shouted.

"Oh, it works," Tom said calmly. "On."

At the word DeVille's body shook momentarily. When the shaking stopped, he collapsed. Tom went over and pulled the shirt away.

"What did you do?" Tina asked. She knelt

next to DeVille and felt his pulse. "It's normal. So why is he unconscious?"

"I rigged the disks," Tom explained. "When I said the word—there's a voice-code chip built into the mesh—they discharged, overloading his nervous system. I would have done it earlier, but then you got in the way, and I didn't want you caught in the jolt."

"Remind me never to get mad at *you*," Tina replied.

"Andy!" Linda called, and she hurled herself into Wellington's arms. "Are you all right? I was so worried."

"Hey, everything's cool," the Duke said, holding her. "My back hurts a little, but I've been hit worse. You know that—" He stopped talking as she kissed him.

The doctor came out of the emergency room, where DeVille had been examined. Robin Montague and two officers had been waiting by the time Tom and the others reached the hospital. Now only Tom remained, and the police chief sat with him while the officers kept watch on DeVille's bed.

"There's no serious damage," the doctor reported.

"In that case," said Chief Montague, "I'd like to take him down to the station."

"Be my guest," the doctor said, and together they went back into the emergency room.

"Tom! Thank goodness you're here!" Sandra Swift cried as she ran into the waiting room. "It was terrible!"

"Sandra," he said. "What's wrong? Why are you here by yourself?"

Before she could answer, a strange feeling came over him, and his blood ran cold. "Oh, no," he gasped. "Something's happened to Rick!"

**13**

YOU HAD TO DO IT, DIDN'T YOU?" SAID TOM. IT was the next morning.

Duke Wellington looked up from his plate. He was seated at a table in the restaurant at the Central Hills Motor Lodge, where he and Johnny Weisel were staying. On his plate was a thick, lean steak and a pile of scrambled eggs, and he paused with his knife slicing through the steak.

"Do what, kid?" Wellington asked Tom. "Had breakfast yet? Sit down and join us, I'll pick up the tab."

"No, thanks," Tom muttered. He was in no mood to let Wellington be nice to him. "Somebody jumped Rick Cantwell. Several guys."

"Gee, that's too bad," Weisel mumbled.

Wellington seemed more concerned. "He's all right, isn't he?"

"Sure," Tom said. "He fought them off. But he's in no condition to fight you in two days."

Weisel sat up with a big, self-satisfied grin. "Now the truth comes out!"

"Johnny . . ." Wellington warned.

Weisel waved him off. "No, Duke, you don't get it. The little nobody is afraid to fight you, so he sends this punk over to cry on our shoulders with some sob story." To Tom he said, "You tell your pal that he fights or he forfeits."

"He was jumped," Tom repeated coldly, "and I think I know why."

Now Wellington got the picture. "Wait a minute! You think *I* had something to do with this?"

Tom's eyes narrowed. "There aren't many other people who'd have a reason to want Rick out of the way."

"I am offended," Weisel protested. "For the Duke, I am offended. How dare you come in here and make accusations like that!"

"My sister was there," Tom told Weisel. "She saw the men who did it run off to a car driven by a round little man who sneered."

Snorting, Weisel slapped his stomach.

"Who're you calling round, punk? Solid muscle, ask anyone." He froze as Wellington glared at him. "Hey, I see what you're saying. Well, it's a lie. I'll sue you for slander! I'll sue you for libel!"

Tom leaned his face very close to Weisel's. "I checked the record books, Weisel. Every time the Duke has a championship fight against really serious competition, something happens to the challenger. Maybe an accident, maybe a fight somewhere, but something always happens. I wonder why."

"He's got a point," Wellington said. "Why'd you have the kid hurt, Johnny? Didn't you think I could win?"

"I didn't do anything!" Weisel blustered. He stood and slapped his napkin down on his plate.

"Then how'd the kid get hurt?" Wellington asked.

"Yours is not to question why," Weisel said. "Yours is to bring home the gold. I like managing a world champion, and I intend to keep it that way."

"You did it," Wellington said. There was no anger in his voice, just a slight edge of disgust and disappointment. Without another word he stood up, turned, and walked off.

"Now look what you've done," Weisel scolded Tom. "He didn't eat his breakfast."

"You're not getting away with this," Tom said.

Weisel chortled. "Get away with what? You're the one with the problem, not me. Your boy's down, so the match is off. Better luck next time."

Tom couldn't think of anything else to say. Weisel was right. He had won. Tom walked away from the table with Weisel's laughter ringing in his ears.

At the door he froze and stood there thinking for a long moment. Then he turned back to Weisel and shouted, "Tell Wellington to get ready—the fight is on!"

Weisel looked up. "What? You haven't got a fighter."

Tom took a deep breath and let it out slowly.

"*I'll* fight him," he said.

"Hit it again, Tom!" Tina yelled. "Harder this time."

Tom drove another kick at the hanging bag. Tina pressed her weight against it from behind to keep it from moving. This time it moved, despite her.

"Much better," she said.

135

Tom wiped the sweat from his brow with a gloved hand. They had been practicing for four hours, and though he was in good shape, he had never been through this kind of concentrated physical effort. The closest thing to it in his experience was the feverish intensity frequently demanded when he was inventing.

After his breakfast confrontation with Weisel and Wellington, Tom had studied all the videotapes, watching again and again as the greatest kickboxers fought their way back and forth across the screen. Even Master Choso was featured and Tina. But though the fight scenes were now part of his growing data base, the valuable experience they recorded, ready to be relayed to his muscles when he needed it, they no longer seemed to be enough. Not against the Duke.

He had needed an edge. Then it had hit him. He needed a trainer. He needed Tina Choso. And Tina had been delighted to oblige.

"Can we take a break?" he asked.

Tina scowled. "Your match is in two days. If you don't want to be ready for it, that's okay with me. I'm not the one who did something really stupid, like force a fight on Duke Wellington."

"If you'd let me use the suit," Tom said, "this would go a lot quicker."

"No!" Tina snapped. "Do you always want to run before you can walk? First you get the basics, and then we talk about the disks." She positioned herself behind the hanging bag again. "Now straight right hand from the chin."

Tom sighed and drew his hand up so that the knuckles were just in front of his lips. He snapped the hand forward, tensing all the muscles in his arm an instant before the glove hit the bag.

"Good," she said. "Uppercut."

He swung his right hand in an arc from his hip, striking the bag as hard as he could.

"Better," said Tina. "You're a quick study, Tom, a real natural. Fast kicks. Four."

*Whomp! Whomp! Whomp! Whomp!* His foot collided with the bag four times.

"We'll have to work on that one. Too slow and not much power."

The session was interrupted by a booming voice over the intercom. "Tom, would it be possible to speak with you?"

"It's Dad!" Tom said. "I didn't know he was home."

"Go see what he wants," replied Tina. She picked up her gear. "You just practice what we've worked on, and I'll see you tomorrow, after school." She darted for the door, but once she had it open, she stopped. "You're the best student I ever had," she said. Then she was out the door.

Tom hurried to his father's office, deep within the complex. He wondered if his father, who had gathered worldwide acclaim for his inventions, had some new creation to show him. But when Tom saw his father, he knew that inventions were not to be the subject of discussion.

Mr. Swift was sitting behind his desk, stroking his chin as if deep in thought. Tom could see concern in his father's piercing blue eyes. When Mr. Swift saw Tom, he hurried out from behind his desk and gave his son a big hug. Tom returned it, and then they took their seats.

"It's good to see you, Dad," Tom said, but he couldn't help noticing the worried look on his father's face.

"It's always good to see you, Tom, you know that, but—" his father began.

"I'm sorry about the helicopter," Tom said.

Tom senior frowned. "You've got the family brains, son, but sometimes I'd swear you don't have the common sense you were born with." He became serious and leaned over the desk. "Anyway, that's not what I called you here for. It's you I'm worried about. You've been busy while I was away."

"Oh," Tom said.

"Are you sure you want to fight Wellington?"

"I've got to do it, Dad. I can't explain it, but I've got to."

His father nodded. "I understand. I remember when I was your age. Everything was so important." He took a deep breath. "But it isn't. Remember that. If things get too rough, you can always walk away from it."

"I'll remember that, Dad."

"I have some other business to attend to, but one last thing. This cybernetic suit you've developed," said Tom senior. "Is it as good as you'd hoped?"

"It's great, Dad," Tom replied. "It's going to change the future of sports."

"We'll see," his father said, which Tom took to mean: Unless it has some practical application outside of sports, it's not leaving your lab again. "When you're finished with what you have to do, I'd like to see the system. If that's all right. The way Sandra described it, I think it may have some interesting properties you've overlooked."

"Sure, Dad," Tom said, and started for the door.

"Tom?"

"Yes, Dad?"

"Good luck."

Tom smiled warmly at his father. "Thanks, Dad." His father, always busy, was already on the phone. He waved goodbye, and Tom closed the door behind him on his way out.

He practiced punches and kicks as he walked down the hall. It was all coming to him too slowly. He had visions of Duke Wellington pounding him into the mat, and he knew what he had to do.

Tina, despite her knowledge of martial arts, was wrong about this. She took her father's viewpoint. That was natural. But neither she nor Master Choso truly understood the significance of his breakthrough.

It was time to use the suit, but not the old suit. Odds were that Weisel wasn't going to let Tom fill the arena with videocameras that would broadcast moves back to Swift Enterprises' central computer so that Tom could counter Wellington properly. No, he reasoned, somehow the disks themselves would have to take the place of cameras.

He ran to his lab. There, on his workbench, was the real suit, not the one he had rigged up for Dangerous Danny DeVille. It was still in pieces, with the disassembled remnants of the black boxes scattered around for parts.

Immediately he threw himself onto his ergonomic chair and started to work on them.

He had an idea. On his computer he brought up a supply list for the Swift complex. A quick scan and he found what he wanted, and minutes after he put his order in, a service robot delivered the package.

Tom carefully picked up an infrared photoreceptor chip and examined it. His father had developed the microscopic chip for use in scanner satellites, but now Tom saw it as a substitute for a videocamera. If he couldn't get a visual fix on Wellington's movements, he could follow them by monitoring the Duke's body heat. Aided by a two-way interface, something else he'd have to build into the disks, the photoreceptors could broadcast directly to the computer, which would be programmed to distinguish his heat patterns from the champ's.

It could work, Tom thought. It had better work.

Tom recalled Rick's experiences with the suit. Rick had resisted it, and when Tom thought back to his own test of the suit, he understood why. Using it was at first like being a robot, a puppet on some distant computer's radiowave string. In his enthusiasm

Tom had ignored the sensation, but now he realized the problem.

Then Rick had kicked into high gear. Why? Nothing about the disks had changed, but Tom had sent a massive jolt of electricity through them. Something had happened then, and he thought he knew what it was.

He attached an electrical lead to the suit and connected a voltameter to measure the strength of the current. Tom gave it a jolt.

The result was impossible. The needle on the voltameter shot as far into the red as it could go and held there. He was right about what had happened to Rick. The disk system, powered by the extra jump, had locked into Rick's electromagnetic field and strengthened it. Rick might have felt like a robot at first, but after the jolt he must have felt as if he were on a runaway roller coaster.

There was no more time to waste. Excited, Tom slipped out of his clothes and into the suit. The fiber-optic fabric was cool against his skin. He held his breath and switched it on. There was a feeling of disorientation, and then a sense of well-being came over him. The suit warmed to skin temperature.

Tom kicked, for practice, and his foot snapped out like a whip. Tom had a feeling of strength that he had never experienced before. He felt confident, energized.

He felt invincible.

"I'm going to win!" he shouted joyfully, and even as he spoke he knew it was no idle boast. It was cold scientific fact, something that had already happened, as far as he was concerned.

"I'll murder the Duke! And then I'll tear apart that little Weisel!"

14

As TOM SWIFT STOOD IN THE LOCKER ROOM of the Jefferson High stadium, he knew it was his night. For the last two days he and Tina had practiced every move, studied every tape, and he was sure there was nothing Duke Wellington could throw at him that he couldn't handle—as long as he was wearing the cybernetic suit.

Tina was still unaware of the extent of his use of what he had now come to think of as his ultra-high-tech cybersuit. Besides the enormous skill and energy it bestowed on him, Tom had noticed other benefits. His left arm, which had ached ever since his battle with Dangerous Danny DeVille on the mountaintop, no longer bothered him. He was completely healed. He felt more alive than he had ever felt before, and he was ready for some serious kickboxing.

Carefully Tom attached the disks to the mesh suit, making sure the optical fibers were undamaged. He made a mental note to investigate the electromagnetic healing effect further. Perhaps that was the other property his father had spoken of.

Duke Wellington appeared with his own gear and took a nearby locker. Tom could see he was uncomfortable. Wellington dressed silently, and several times he cast his eyes on Tom and looked as if he were going to speak. Finally Wellington said, "I just want you to know I had nothing to do with that attack on your friend."

Tom didn't reply.

"You were right, Johnny was behind it," Wellington continued. "After tonight he's through as my manager. I may not be the best person in the world, but I draw the line at jumping kids."

Tom remained silent.

"Got a problem, kid?" Wellington said, exasperated. "We worked well together against DeVille, so I'm willing to give you a shot to prove your system's as good as you think it is. I figure I owe you. But you aren't walking out of here with my belt, no matter what."

"I'm going to make you wish you'd never seen me," Tom said. The threat startled even him.

The Duke's eyes narrowed. "That'll be easy. I already do." He stormed out, leaving Tom alone again.

Why did I say that? Tom wondered. That wasn't like me at all. He remembered Rick's strange behavior, and an unsettling suspicion began to gnaw at him.

Could it be the cybersuit? Did the impulses it sent along the nervous system also affect personality and conduct? It was something he intended to investigate, but first he had a match to win.

Tom slipped on his boxing gloves and left the dressing room. Outside the door Sandra and Rick waited. Rick balanced himself on a crutch.

"How's the leg?" Tom asked.

"As long as I stay off it, it'll be great in a couple of days," Rick said. "Let's get you down to ringside."

As they approached the ring, Tom looked around. The stadium was packed. He recognized many of his neighbors from Central

Hills, but the front rows were filled with strangers. Rick pointed them out one by one, the cream of the sport of kickboxing. Linda Nueve had camerapeople scattered outside the ring, ready to record and transmit footage of the match. Linda herself was seated in the front row, next to Master Choso. Tina, smiling confidently, stood in Tom's corner of the ring.

"Good luck, slugger," Sandra called out as she and Rick took their seats next to Master Choso. Luck, Tom knew, would have nothing to do with it. The only pivotal factor in this match was science, and it was on his side.

"Ready?" Tina asked as Tom climbed onto the ring apron. In the opposite corner Duke Wellington stood and glowered at Tom, while Johnny Weisel rubbed the champ's shoulders, limbering him up. Weisel scowled, staring daggers at both Tom and the Duke.

"Ready, willing, and able," Tom replied. He ran a finger down an optical fiber. He felt charged. Everything was set.

Later, what happened next would be a blur to Tom. Spotlights beat down on him, warming him. A ring announcer read off his name and Wellington's, and he could hear the cheers of the crowd when they heard his. Tina made a comment, pointing out Wellington's possible weaknesses. All this Tom was aware of, but his attention was now completely focused on Wellington and the fight ahead. In Wellington's corner Weisel gave him a sip of water, and then Wellington's mouth guard went in.

The bell rang, and Tom and the Duke moved to the center of the ring. They tapped gloves, and Wellington said, "Have yourself a ball, kid."

Tom said, "On." The cybernetic exoskeleton powered up.

Before Tom knew it, Wellington drove a left hook at his body. For a moment terror overwhelmed him. Then his elbows moved in, blocking the blow.

The heat receptors work! Tom realized. The computer back at the Swift labs was able to read the Duke's movements just as if they were on video.

Tom kicked sharply, snapping two blows into Wellington's knee. The Duke went off his footing, rolled sideways along his shoulder, and came up in a crouch, warier than ever.

They danced around each other, sparring with occasional kicks and punches. Tom parried Wellington's moves with ease, and he could tell the champ was getting frustrated.

Tom punched with a straight right. Wellington caught it and spun, driving an elbow into Tom's left shoulder. Tom jerked back in pain as his injury flared up.

Then the pain was gone in an electromagnetic burst. A sense of well-being flooded through Tom. He executed a flying kick that harmlessly glanced off Wellington's chest.

Wellington was in midpunch when the bell rang, sounding the end of the first round. To Tom's surprise, the punch stopped at the instant they heard the bell. It reminded him of DeVille. But even the Dangerous One did not possess the precise muscle control of the Duke.

Right then Tom was overwhelmed with admiration for Wellington's skills. Whatever the man had allowed himself to become, he was clearly a master of his art.

"You're hanging in there just fine," Tina said as Tom got back to his corner. He hung on the ropes as she rubbed his shoulders, loosening him up. "Keep it up, stay out of his reach, and you may survive this."

"Next round I break him," Tom said. Again, the threat surprised him. It was as if someone else were speaking through his mouth.

"Have you learned what you wanted to learn?" said a voice from the floor. Tom turned his head to see Master Choso standing there.

"Yes, my disks work great," Tom said.

Master Choso smiled his crafty smile. "And what have you learned of yourself? In your science, where is the art?"

Tom felt the master's words as hot needles jabbing at him. He became infuriated. "I don't see Wellington worrying an awful lot about art *or* philosophy!"

Choso's face darkened. "Yes. One of my finest students and one of my greatest failures. I passed to him my skills, but . . ." His words trailed off, as if he were deep in thought, and then he snapped his head up, his eyes boring deep into Tom's. "Still, I sense in him a nobility struggling to assert itself. He helped you when he had nothing to gain by it. Despite the way he has lived and fought, he has kept faith with bargains he and I have made. What will *you* keep faith with, Tom Swift? What?"

Tom puzzled over the master's words. Sometimes, he thought, that man doesn't make a bit of sense. The bell rang, catching Tom's attention. When he looked back, Master Choso was gone.

Tom and the Duke hit the center of the ring at the same time. Wellington swung a high, wide kick at Tom's head. Tom ducked deep under it and sprang back up, with an uppercut to Wellington's ribs. The champ dropped an elbow on Tom's shoulder.

Tom rolled away. Wellington followed him across the ring with a series of low kicks that kept Tom from fighting back. His muscles flinched and tensed as he rolled again and again, and still he was filled with admiration for Wellington. The man had taken what he knew of how the disks worked and used that to force Tom into a totally defensive position. The computer that managed Tom's maneuvers would be locked into backing him out of danger, leaving Wellington to trick Tom into the kickboxing equivalent of checkmate.

Then a strange thing happened. In the midst of his attack the Duke wavered. He stumbled back, legs rubbery for a moment, and wiped at his eyes. Tom sprang to his feet and drove a kick into Wellington's chest. The champ wobbled. Tom twisted, driving the back of his hand into Wellington's back. The blow had little effect, but the Duke made no attempt to retaliate. He stared off at nothing, as though he had forgotten he was in the ring.

With a shout Tom swung at Wellington with a roundhouse right. Meekly Wellington watched the punch connect, and his legs buckled. Tom had put him on the mat.

The champ was down, and a thrill of excitement shot through Tom. As he stood over the fallen Duke, he wanted to gloat—and in that instant Tom understood. He knew what Choso meant by keeping faith, and in his heart he knew the teacher was right. This was supposed to be a test of his own skill, his limits and endurance, but Tom had cheated himself of all that. His cybersuit was a shortcut to an end that was meant to be achieved slowly. There was no achievement in what he was doing. There was only the fight and the unsettling thrill he was getting from it.

Tom couldn't remember ever taking joy in inflicting pain on another person. It was against his nature. Yet here he was, doing exactly that. As the realization hit home, he knew there was only one thing he could do.

"Off," Tom said. The suit powered down. He was on his own, facing one of the toughest men on the planet.

Wellington got up and shook the haze from his eyes. He focused on Tom again, and Tom raised his fists, preparing for the Duke's onslaught.

The champ staggered forward, swinging wildly. Tom backed away from the punches and ran into the ropes. Wellington was on him, hugging him in a clinch. Wellington's face was damp with sweat, and his eyes were blearier than Tom expected. His skin was cold and clammy.

Tom easily broke the clinch and backed away from the wobbly Duke. Then Tom understood. Something was wrong with Wellington.

He had to stop the fight.

Tom turned to the referee, but before he could speak, a glove smacked him alongside the ear. His balance momentarily thrown off by the blow, Tom dropped to the mat. Wellington swung a roundhouse kick into Tom's side with such force that it rolled Tom completely over. Dropping to one knee, the Duke jabbed down with a fierce punch aimed straight between Tom's eyes.

Tom rolled just before the blow connected and countered with a backhand punch that caught Wellington square in the nose. Wellington stood up, dazed, holding his nose with one glove. He teetered back. Tom got into position for a kick, but Wellington was no longer paying attention to him. The Duke's eyes wandered, glancing over the crowd.

Then he toppled forward on his face and lay still.

A hush fell over the audience. As the crowd watched, Weisel scurried into the ring and got to Wellington's side.

"Duke!" he shouted, but Wellington didn't respond. He patted his face. Nothing. Weisel rolled the champ over and put his ear to Wellington's chest.

When Weisel raised his head again, his face was white with horror. He shoved an accusing finger at Tom.

"He's dead!" Weisel screamed. "You killed him!"

I T'S NOT POSSIBLE!" TOM BLURTED. "I COULDN'T
have killed him! I barely touched him!"

But no one was listening. Weisel was on his
knees, clutching Wellington to him, playing
to the crowd with tears in his eyes.

"He killed him!" Weisel shouted. "Look!"

Weisel held up Wellington's limp hand,
already turning blue at the fingertips. "Proof!
Proof that he gave the champ an electric
shock with that—that machine of his!"

"I couldn't have," Tom said. "I switched it
off before he fell."

By then Tina had entered the ring. Over
Weisel's protests, she shoved the chubby
manager aside. Tina set Wellington's head on

the floor and pressed open an eye with her thumb.

"His pupils are dilated," she said. "He's definitely in shock."

"I can guarantee it wasn't electricity that caused it," Tom said. "But what—?"

"His lips and his fingers are turning blue," Tina said. "There are some poisons that do that. They cut off oxygen."

Tom mulled that over for a second. "And Weisel was giving the Duke water before the match. . . ."

He turned to see Weisel scurry to Wellington's corner. The manager was already reaching for the water bottle.

"Stop him!" Tom yelled. By the time Tom could reach him, he would have the contents of the water bottle spilled all over the stadium floor.

Weisel turned the bottle upside down with the open end of the built-in plastic straw hovering above the ground.

A drop trickled out, and then the flow stopped.

Tom laughed. He recognized the design of the straw. It was for use by astronauts, with a valve that kept liquids in the bottle unless suction pulled them out.

Tom lunged for the manager.

Desperately Weisel pried at the cap. It didn't budge. Then Master Choso was at the manager's side. A swift kick sent the bottle flying from Weisel's hand. It landed in Tom's gloves as if it had been aimed there.

"Wellington told me he gave Weisel notice," Tom said. "He wasn't going to use him as his manager anymore."

"Is that reason enough to try to kill him?" asked Tina.

"Ask him," Tom said, pointing an accusing finger at Weisel.

"It was a joke!" Weisel screamed. "He has the constitution of an ox. How was I supposed to know he couldn't take it?"

Weisel turned to the crowd, and his terror grew at the sight of their angry faces. "Don't you humanoids get it? He was nothing without me! I made him what he is today. He had no right to fire me! He's a lousy ingrate!"

Weisel looked to his left. Master Choso was slowly closing in on him. Ahead of him Linda Nueve's crew had him in their camera sights.

"Make sure you get everything he says," Linda angrily told them. Frantic at the sight of Wellington lying on the mat, she shoved her way past Weisel and climbed into the ring.

Weisel shook a fist at her, but the boos from

the crowd reminded him of his situation. If he stayed where he was, in moments he would be a caged animal. He ran.

"Have a nice trip," said a familiar voice.

His feet tangled on something, and he hit the floor. Rough hands lifted him up. His jaw dropped.

He was staring into the face of Rick Cantwell, who was seated in the first row.

"I figure I owed you something," Rick said, holding up his crutch.

"I didn't mean to!" Johnny Weisel hollered as security guards hauled him away. "It's all a big mistake! I wouldn't hurt the Duke—or anyone! We're pals! Buddies! You've got to believe me!"

In the ring Linda Nueve crouched next to Tina Choso. "How is he?" she asked.

Tina shook her head sadly. "I don't think he's going to make it."

"We can get him to a hospital."

"There's no time," Tina insisted. "If he isn't treated now—"

"I've got an idea," Tom said. He yanked off his gloves and began to peel off the exoskeleton.

"What are you doing?" asked Tina, bewildered.

"You'll see," Tom said. "Just help me with this."

Quickly they got him out of it, and as Tom started to wrap a sleeve around the Duke's arm, he explained, "His system's failing, that's the problem. This should link into his personal electromagnetic field, and with any luck it will strengthen him enough to fight off the poison."

Linda Nueve and Tina gazed at him, completely bewildered.

"Trust me," Tom said.

When the cybernetic mesh completely covered Wellington's upper arm, Tom said, "On." Wellington's body shook slightly as a charge rippled through it.

Tom could almost see the energy condensing around the Duke. There was just one problem—it wasn't working. Wellington wasn't getting any better.

"He's fading fast!" Tina cried. "I don't know what to do."

"Duke!" Linda shouted. "Don't you dare leave me again. Not now." It was no use.

"I'll be back," Tom said. He hurried out of the ring and went running for the locker room.

"Where are you going?" Tina called frantically.

"Just keep him alive until I get back," said Tom.

He reached his locker and yanked it open. There, on the bottom shelf where he had left it, was his portable computer. It was on automatic program, monitoring his responses. Tom grabbed the computer and raced back to the ring.

"Uncle Andy's breathing is a lot shallower," Tina told him when he arrived. "If you're going to do something, you'd better do it quickly."

"I need information—age, height, weight, that sort of thing," Tom began, and he rattled off a battery of questions. Tina and Linda answered them as best they could.

Tom ran a program correlating the data and testing, through the disks, the electrical resistance level of Duke Wellington's skin.

"Look at these readings," Tom said in awe. "No wonder the exoskeleton wasn't having any effect. It was set for *my* readings. Giving him the current I took is like sending houseflies against a rhino."

He adjusted the settings and crossed his fingers.

A surge of energy passed through the Duke. The optical fibers hummed from disk to disk. Wellington gave no response.

I've failed, Tom thought. He felt numb. Linda, who had been watching him for signs of hope, sadly sank her face into the Duke's chest.

It was over.

Slowly Tom folded down the lid of his laptop, trying to figure out where his calculations had gone wrong.

"Look!" said Tina. As Tom watched, she raised Wellington's slack hand.

The Duke's fingers were no longer blue. His lips, too, had regained their color. His breathing was returning to normal.

"That's it!" said Tom. "That's the part of the equation I forgot to figure in—time."

Wellington's eyes fluttered open. He studied the faces looking down on him and, with a weak grin, mumbled, "Can't a guy take a little nap around here?"

Tom knocked on the door of Master Choso's dojo. Sounds of a party came from inside, and Tom was glad. After everything that had happened, he was ready for some fun.

"Tom," said Tina as she opened the door. "Come on in. I just spoke to Rick and Sandra. They're on their way over, and the guests of honor are already here."

He stepped inside and looked around.

Instead of the usual bare walls, the dojo was trimmed in balloons and bright streamers. Dance music blared from a stereo.

"Have you heard the good news?" Tina continued. "Uncle Andy's well enough to leave Central Hills, and he and Aunt Linda wanted to thank everyone."

"Aunt Linda?"

Tina giggled. "She said I should call her that."

"Hey, Swifty!" shouted a deep voice. Duke Wellington greeted Tom with a smile and a bear hug. Entering the room a few steps behind the Duke were Linda Nueve and Master Choso.

"Hi, Duke," Tom grunted as the wind was squeezed out of him. When Wellington let him go, he added, "What was that Swifty stuff?"

"If you're going to be a kickboxer, you have to have a good name, something the people will remember. I thought Swifty Swift sounded good."

Tom rolled his eyes. "Sorry, Duke, I'm getting out of the game. But thanks, anyway."

With a grin Wellington pulled Linda to him and wrapped a big arm around her. "Too bad. You throw quite a kick. If you ever decide to go pro, I can recommend a manager. The best." Tom could see from the way they looked at each other that the Duke was talking about Linda.

"That's great," Tom replied. "Linda, you're his manager now? What about the sportscasting gig?"

"I'm giving that up," she said. "That was just something I did until I could get this big goof to see things my way. He originally asked me to be his manager when he won the title from Choso, but then that little cockroach Weisel started whispering all sorts of lies and promises to him."

"I think," Wellington said, "I was scared. I was afraid I wouldn't measure up. And there's always that nagging fear that the next guy's the one who's going to take you down." He chuckled. "I guess I needed taking down, at least a peg or two."

"Well, it looks like your worries are over now. Congratulations," Tom said, and he shook hands with Linda and the Duke. Out of the corner of his eye he saw Master Choso signal. "Excuse me, okay?"

He followed Master Choso into the back room. The master closed the door and said, "I owe you an apology."

"I owe you—" Tom began, but Master Choso raised a hand to silence him.

"I was wrong to assume that my style and methods are better than yours. That is a judgment no man should make. Our ways are different, that is all, and perhaps"—he gave Tom a wink—"perhaps there is much we can learn from each other, eh?"

"One thing I'd like to know," Tom said. "Did you really let Wellington beat you for the title?"

The master pondered a long time before answering. "When Andrew Wellington was my student, I saw in him the seeds of a brave and noble man. But he resisted his own character. Like you, he sought shortcuts that would bring him to his goal more quickly. Unlike you, he chose a negative path.

"I tried many ways to bring him back. Finally, I became tired with the world of competition. In one more attempt to steer him to the correct path, I arranged to surrender the world title to Andrew, in the hopes that the attainment of his goal would finally allow him to open up to himself. It didn't. He became even more arrogant and suspicious of everyone around him. He surrounded himself with evil."

"You mean Johnny Weisel," Tom interjected.

"And others," Choso answered. "But Andrew and I had a pact. In exchange for the belt he must visit me regularly, and I would be able to ask of him a single favor, which he was forbidden to refuse. If he had broken that pact, I would have known he was lost forever. In keeping it he proved there was still honor in him somewhere, waiting to be drawn out. Your friend Rick always spoke quite highly of you. I thought you might make an excellent student—if you could be weaned from your dependence on technology. And the annoying American habit of wanting everything yesterday," he added with a sly smile.

Tom snapped his fingers. "You set me up! And here I thought it was all my idea!"

"It was both of us," Choso replied, "each of us working toward the same end, with our own ways and for our own reasons."

Tom grinned and bowed. "Master Choso, I would be honored to study the martial arts with you and learn them properly."

With a broad smile Master Choso returned the bow. "And I would be honored to learn from you . . . Master Swift."

They laughed, and Choso led him back to the party.

Rick had arrived with Sandra. He was back on his feet, the crutch already forgotten. "Did you hear about Weisel and DeVille?" he said when he saw Tom. "Looks like they'll be sharing a cell. Hey, sorry about the exoskeleton."

Tom shrugged. "Dad's got his people working on it. It could be a big deal in medicine, if they can ever get around the personality warp." Then Tom's face clouded. "Rick," he said, "I want to apologize for foolishly putting your life in danger. I knew the cybersuit was affecting your judgment. I let my impatience to perfect it cloud my own judgment."

"Yeah," Rick said. "Boy, I can't believe I was rushing so eagerly toward the most dangerous fight of my life."

Tom smiled grimly. "We both were."

"I guess that's it for you and sports inventions for a while, right?"

Even as Rick spoke, ideas started clicking in Tom's head.

"Uh-oh," Sandra said. "Somebody hide the solar soldering iron. He's got that look on his face again."

"Rick," Tom said, putting an arm around his friend and walking him away from the others, "tell me everything you know about football. . . ."

## Tom's next adventure:

Tom Swift's latest invention has set off an evolution revolution in reverse. His microradiation DNA scanner, destabilized by a black hole created in an earlier experiment, has created a biological time warp. Now the scanner's beam of alien energy threatens to put the entire world into prehistoric peril.

A house cat is transformed into a ferocious saber-toothed tiger . . . a mynah bird becomes a carnivorous flying reptile . . . and Tom's friend Rick devolves into a rampaging ape-man. Tom must find a way to defuse the DNA time bomb before a savage new Stone Age explodes into being . . . in Tom Swift #4, *The DNA Disaster*.